The Walking Scarecrow

In the moonlight Frank and Joe could see a tall figure standing between the cornstalks.

The man wore a tall stovepipe hat, and a tattered black coat and pants. His black eyes glared at the boys over a long, curved nose, and his face was ghastly white. His mouth was twisted in a cruel grin. His long arms were extended, and the fingers were curved like the talons of a bird of prey.

"It's a scarecrow!" Frank exploded. "We've been talking to a scarecrow!"

The boys started to walk away when they heard an eerie warning.

"Beware! Leave this place and flee for your lives!"

The Hardys stood rooted to the spot. Frank's hair rose on the back of his neck. Joe felt goosebumps. The scarecrow had just spoken to them!

The Hardy Boys Mystery Stories

**Available from MINSTREL Books
and ALADDIN Paperbacks**

GHOST STORIES

THE HARDY BOYS®

FRANKLIN W. DIXON

Aladdin Paperbacks
New York London Toronto Sydney Singapore

This book is a work of fiction. Any references to historical events,
real people, or real locales are used fictitiously. Other names,
characters, places, and incidents are the product of the author's
imagination, and any resemblance to actual events or locales
or persons, living or dead, is entirely coincidental.

First Aladdin Paperbacks edition May 2002
First Minstrel edition July 1987
First Wanderer Books Edition 1984

ALADDIN PAPERBACKS
An imprint of Simon & Schuster
Children's Publishing Division
1230 Avenue of the Americas
New York, NY 10020

Printed in the U.S.A.

23 22 21 20 19 18 17 16 15

THE HARDY BOYS and THE HARDY BOYS MYSTERY
STORIES are trademarks of Simon & Schuster, Inc.

ISBN 0-671-69133-3

Library of Congress Control Number: 83-16953

CONTENTS

FOREWORD

Dear Fans,

Frank and Joe Hardy are well known as excellent detectives. They have used their sharp sleuthing skills to solve many difficult and baffling cases.

In this book of ghost stories I have presented the Hardys with a new challenge—the supernatural! Ordinarily our young sleuths would never believe in ghosts, but the eerie happenings in these tales keep them guessing.

I have a hunch my stories will keep you guessing, too. But beware, you just might begin to believe in ghosts yourself!

Franklin W. Dixon

THE
WALKING
SCARECROW

"Joe, there's something wrong with the engine!" Eighteen-year-old Frank Hardy sounded exasperated. He and his younger brother were driving home after a day of backpacking in Bayport Hills. They were still out in the countryside and night was falling. All they could see under a rising full moon were tall cornstalks on either side of the bumpy dirt road.

Frank stepped on the gas, but the engine refused to respond.

Joe shook his blond head. "We sure don't need a breakdown here. We're a zillion miles from nowhere!"

But the motor gave a last *ping-ping-ping* and then stopped altogether. Frank used their momentum to guide the sports sedan into a ditch by the side of the road. With the help of a flashlight, the boys worked over the engine for some time, but to no avail.

"It's no use. We'll need a tow," Frank said at last. "But where do we get one out here in the boondocks?"

Joe looked around. "I think we're in luck, Frank. That must be the farmer over there. Maybe he'll give us a tow or let us call the nearest garage."

Joe pointed across the road, and in the moonlight Frank could see a tall figure standing between the cornstalks.

"Let's catch him before he goes home," Joe urged.

Frank agreed. They crossed the road and tramped through rugged furrows where the ground had been plowed. Finally they arrived at the spot in the middle of the cornfield, where the farmer stood.

The moon was about to vanish behind a cloud, but they could still see enough to be startled.

The man wore a tall, stovepipe hat, tattered black coat and pants, and long shoes with upturned toes. His black eyes glared at the boys over a long, curved nose, and his face was ghastly white. His mouth was twisted in a cruel grin. His long arms were extended and the fingers were curved like the talons of a bird of prey.

Joe shuddered and Frank felt cold chills run down his spine. Both boys instinctively moved back between the corn.

Just then the moon disappeared. Darkness covered the field, and they strained their eyes to see the eerie figure. "This guy's a weirdo," Joe mumbled. "I bet he lives in a haunted house!"

2

"He's the only person around," Frank whispered. "He's got to help us!"

He stepped forward and called out, "Sir, our car broke down. We need a tow."

.There was no answer. A rising wind ruffled the corn tassels. Frank and Joe waited with pounding hearts and tense nerves.

"We'd better stay where we are," Frank warned in an undertone. "We don't know who this guy is. Maybe he's off his rocker! If we turn, he might jump us!"

"But where is he?" Joe hissed. "It's so dark, he could be behind us by now!" The boy glanced over his shoulder as he spoke.

Suddenly the cloud drifted past. Moonlight flooded the cornfield again and the sinister figure came into clear view.

Now the Hardys could see that it was attached to a pole thrust into the ground between two corn furrows. Wisps of straw poked out from under the hat. The fingers were made of wire. The face was painted on.

"It's a scarecrow!" Frank exploded. "We've been talking to a scarecrow!"

"It sure looks real," Joe responded. "I wonder who made it? It gives me the creeps!"

"Me, too, Joe. But there should be a farmhouse around here. Let's try there."

The boys started walking away when they heard an eerie warning.

"Beware! Leave this place and flee for your lives!"

The Hardys stood rooted to the spot. Frank's hair rose on the back of his neck. Joe felt goose bumps. They stared speechlessly at the scarecrow. It had spoken!

The wind fluttered its clothing, and its upturned toes moved. Its grin seemed to mock the boys in the moonlight, while the talonlike fingers appeared to be reaching for them!

"Joe, did you hear what I heard?" Frank asked hoarsely.

"I sure did," Joe replied. "But scarecrows don't talk!"

"Let's try again. Maybe we can solve this mystery."

This time Frank spoke to the scarecrow. "Why do you say we should leave? What kind of danger are we in?"

The scarecrow just glared at them.

Frank asked a few more questions without getting a reply. Nothing broke the silence except the moaning of the wind in the corn.

"That does it!" Frank muttered. "We're wasting our time. Come on, Joe!"

"I'm with you," Joe confessed with a shudder. "But which way do we go?"

Gazing around the area, Frank spotted a large building looming in the distance on the other side of the cornfield.

"That must be the farmhouse," he noted. "Let's try there."

"Sure. Any place is better than here," Joe agreed.

The Hardys turned away from the scarecrow and

began to walk across the cornfield in the direction of the house. It was slow going because the drifting clouds occasionally darkened the moon. The footing was treacherous. They stumbled over mounds of earth thrown up by the plow and stubbed their toes on fallen cornstalks.

"This is worse than backpacking!" Joe puffed as he jumped from one furrow to another.

"I'd rather climb Bayport Hills," Frank agreed.

Just then Joe heard a furtive noise. Stealthy footsteps were sneaking after them!

He nudged Frank with his elbow. "We're being followed," he warned in a low voice.

"I hear it, too," Frank whispered. "Let's set up an ambush!"

The Hardys walked ten paces forward without turning their heads. They listened to the sneaky footsteps dogging them through the cornfield. On the count of ten, they spun around and went into a defensive karate stance.

They were ready to tackle their pursuer. But they saw nothing in the semidarkness of the clouded moon. The sound of the footsteps had ceased.

Frank grimaced. "We must be getting jumpy, Joe. We're imagining things."

"Maybe it was just the wind in the corn," Joe said halfheartedly. "Anyway, who would be out here following us?"

He had barely spoken when a couple of large cornstalks were pushed apart violently. The moon, reappearing from behind a cloud, shone on the ghastly white face of the scarecrow, as the weird creature grinned mockingly at them in the moon-light!

Frank and Joe were mesmerized by the sight. They stood stock-still and stared at the apparition, which was crouched down in a furrow holding the stalks apart. It kept grinning.

Suddenly it emitted a grisly laugh—a terrifying sound in the stillness of the night. The laughter rose to a high point and broke off.

Then the scarecrow spoke to them for a second time. "Do not go to the house!" it rasped. "Leave here or it will be the worse for you!"

The Hardys stood there, doubting their senses. The scarecrow released the cornstalks and allowed them to snap together. The gruesome face vanished, and the sound of retreating footsteps could be heard.

The young detectives came to with a start. They ran to the spot where the scarecrow had been and peered around. But they saw and heard nothing.

"Let's follow it!" Frank exclaimed.

"Which way?"

"Back to the place where we first saw it!"

The boys retraced their footsteps as rapidly as possible, and soon reached the spot where they had confronted the scarecrow.

The pole was bare and the creature was gone!

Frank and Joe were thunderstruck. They felt their hearts pounding furiously.

"Joe, are we seeing things?" Frank asked in a shaky voice.

"And hearing things?" Joe wondered. He shook his head as if to clear it of cobwebs.

The Walking Scarecrow

Rousing themselves from their momentary indecision, they scouted around the area. But they found nothing, and decided to continue on to the house for help.

"Maybe the farmer can tell us something about his walking scarecrow," Joe suggested hopefully.

A long trek brought them to the building, a large, rambling wooden structure towering above a grove of trees. There was no light in any of the windows.

Joe led the way up the steps to the porch. He pressed the doorbell, and they heard a shrill noise inside the house. But nobody answered! Joe rang a few more times. Still there was no response.

"Sounds like no one's home," Frank said. "But we can't go away without making sure."

"Somebody could be at the back of the house," Joe agreed. "Let's find out."

They descended from the porch to the ground and walked around the building, looking for a sign of light as they went. But there was nothing. Tangled underbrush clutched at their feet. They pushed aside brambles that pricked their hands and swatted at mosquitoes buzzing about their ears.

"This stuff hasn't been mowed since the year one," Frank complained.

Before Joe could comment, an unearthly screech made them freeze in their tracks.

"What was that?" Joe burst out.

"I hope it wasn't the scarecrow," Frank muttered.

They heard a fluttering of wings in the nearest tree. An owl flew down and perched on a bush. Its big round eyes glared at them. Ruffling its feathers, it screeched again.

The Hardys grinned ruefully at each other. Relaxing, they completed their tour around the house, and reached the porch again without noticing any sign of life inside. They shouted loudly and got no reply.

"This is an emergency," Joe declared. "We've got to use the phone to call a garage. Anyone would say we had a right to go in."

"Any port in a storm," Frank agreed. He tried the door and found it bolted. The windows, too, refused to budge when he tried to open them.

"The other windows are too high to get at," he said in a disappointed tone.

Joe shook his head. "There's one chance, Frank. When that screech owl flew down at us, I noticed that a branch of the tree was close to the attic window. If the window's open, we should be able to get in."

They went back to the tree. Joe wound his arms around the trunk and shinnied up. Testing the higher branches to be sure they would hold his weight, he climbed until he was on the branch that extended toward the window.

Gingerly inching his way outward, he reached a point where he could press his hand against the glass. The window moved inward under the pressure, as the hinges squeaked spookily.

"We're in luck," Joe called down. "It's unlocked! Come on up."

Frank swarmed up the tree and joined Joe on the

branch. Having got the window open all the way, the younger Hardy clambered over the sill into the attic. Frank came right after him. Once inside, they took pencil flashlights from their detective kits.

Shining the beams around, they realized they were in a large, empty room with rafters overhead. Dust lay thick on the floor.

"No footprints," Frank observed. "Nobody's been up here in a long time."

Joe flickered his light across the attic. "Well, there's the door, Frank. We sure won't find a phone up here. Let's go downstairs."

As they moved across the room, a weird chattering broke out over their heads. Black forms swooped down on them from the rafters. Instinctively Frank and Joe hit the floor. The attackers veered away, returned to their perches on the rafters, and resumed their chattering.

"Bats!" Joe exploded. Dozens of 'em. Let's get out of here fast!"

"Stay down and keep moving," Frank advised.

The Hardys slithered across the attic floor in a panther crawl. Reaching the door, they hastily opened it, crept through, and closed it behind them.

They went down the stairs, found another door, and went through into the hall on the upper floor of the house.

"You know something?" Frank said. "I think this is an abandoned building. There's no carpet on the floor, no furniture in the hall, and no light bulbs anywhere!"

A noise in the room at the head of the hall made him break off. The Hardys flattened themselves against the wall and slipped along to the door, which they found ajar. Frank pushed it open and they played their flashlights inside. The room was empty.

Frank turned his beam downward to the floor. "There's the one who made the noise!" He laughed.

A rat scurried away and escaped into a hole in one of the floorboards.

The Hardys checked the rest of the rooms on the upper floor, each taking one side of the hall.

"I've come up with nothing," Joe declared when they met and compared notes.

"Neither have I. I wonder what it's like on the ground floor?"

They went down the stairs and turned into the dining room, which was bare and dusty like the rest of the house.

But then they spotted footprints.

"Somebody's been here!" Frank exclaimed in a startled tone.

"And not long ago!" Joe gulped.

They followed the prints with their flashlights. The marks led them into the kitchen and across to the back door, which was locked. A second set of footprints guided them into the middle of the living room.

"Only one person made these tracks," Joe noted. "He came in through the back door and went out the same way."

Frank gasped as he flicked his light across the

floor. "Joe, those are bits of straw over there. Either somebody's been pitching hay in this room or the scarecrow has been here!"

Joe shivered. "Suppose it's in the house right now, maybe in the basement! We'd better find out what's going on!"

"That's for sure," Frank answered grimly.

Returning to the kitchen, they found more footprints leading to the basement door and down a flight of steps. At the bottom of the stairs the Hardys paused and looked around apprehensively. The basement was as bare as the rest of the house. Dust covered the furnace and air conditioner. Spiderwebs crisscrossed the windows. There was no door to the yard.

The footprints continued over to the fuse box. Frank examined it and reported that the electricity was turned off and all the fuses were gone. "The footprints go back to the stairs," he added.

Making their way upstairs, Frank and Joe held a council of war.

"There's no phone," Frank noted. "So we can't call for a tow."

Joe shrugged. "We have two choices. We can go back and wait in the car. Or we can spend the night here. I vote we stay inside. We can sleep on the floor."

Frank stretched and yawned. "I agree. We might as well make ourselves comfortable. It's not midnight yet and we can catch a few hours of shut-eye."

He took off his jacket, rolled it up, lay down on

the floor, and placed it under his head for a pillow. Joe did the same. Almost immediately they fell asleep in the darkness and silence of the big house.

The excitement they had experienced since their car had broken down caused them both to have eerie nightmares involving the scarecrow.

Frank dreamed he and Joe were driving in search of a big house. They lost their way, and decided to ask for directions. But all the pedestrians were surly. None would answer their questions.

Suddenly a weird voice behind the Hardys said, "The house is to the right. Make the turn and speed up!"

Glancing over his shoulder, Frank was astounded to see the scarecrow in the back seat!

The apparition grinned at him scornfully. It tipped its stovepipe hat and added, "There is no need to ask anyone else. I will give you directions to the house. Go to the right!"

But Frank knew that to the right was a steep cliff, so he spun the wheel to the left. Yet the car turned right. He stepped on the brake to slow down, but instead the car picked up speed! Terrified, the Hardys continued on a direct course toward the cliff. On and on they went—faster and faster!

The scarecrow in the back seat began to snicker. Just then, the car hurtled over the edge of the cliff. It flew through the air and took a heart-stopping nose dive toward the rocks far below. Down and down it fell! Frank saw the rocks getting bigger and bigger!

The scarecrow gave a demented shriek of triumph. Frank placed his hands over his ears and waited for the car to crash violently into the rocks.

At that point, he woke up. It took him a moment before he realized where he was.

What a nightmare! he thought. The scarecrow must really be getting to me.

Suddenly a floorboard groaned on the porch, and footsteps approached the front window. Sitting up, Frank saw the scarecrow peering at him! A twisted grin distorted its features.

"Am I still dreaming?" Frank gasped. "Or is it for real?"

The apparition spoke to him in a hoarse whisper. "Leave this house at once! This is your last warning!"

Suddenly the creature pulled away from the window and vanished.

Frank jumped to his feet and ran to the door. He had to struggle to force the bolt back because it was clogged with dust. Then he rushed out onto the porch and looked around.

Joe came after him a few seconds later. "You woke me up when you pushed the bolt," he said. "What's going on?"

Quickly Frank explained what had happened. "I don't know where the scarecrow is," he concluded.

"There it is!" Joe exploded.

He pointed toward the field, where the eerie figure was standing next to the first row of corn. The moonlight was bright enough to reveal an ugly scowl on its face.

"Come with me!" it screamed at them.

Then it plunged through the cornstalks into the field.

"We have to follow it!" Joe exclaimed. "Otherwise we may never find out what's going on here!"

"We'll corner it, don't worry," Frank vowed.

They ran to the place where the scarecrow had disappeared. Heavy thunderclouds were building up in the night sky, and the treetops waved wildly in the wind.

The boys entered the cornfield and came to the scarecrow's pole. It was empty!

Frank shrugged in despair. "How can we follow this thing when we don't know where it has gone? The way it disappears is creepy. And then it pops up when we least expect it."

"Let's split up and take different routes through the cornfield," Joe advised.

"Good idea. You go to the right, and I'll move left. Yell if you see anything. And if I call, come on the double."

"Will do," Joe agreed.

He went down the furrow to the right, and then turned at an angle deeper into the cornfield. He walked carefully, pushing the stalks apart and surveying the area before proceeding onward.

A peal of thunder sounded in the distance, and jagged bolts of lightning flashed across the night sky. Moonlight filtering through the clouds caused shadows to flicker around the cornfield. Fantastic shapes danced before Joe's eyes.

"It's a great night for a ghost," he muttered softly to himself. "A real witches' sabbath!"

The Walking Scarecrow

Pushed by a strong wind, the clouds drifted away from the moon and suddenly light flooded the cornfield again.

A piece of cloth fluttering from a stalk caught Joe's attention. When he retrieved it, he saw that it was from a tattered black coat like the one worn by the scarecrow.

Our friend must have come this way, the young detective reasoned. Maybe he's hiding in the corn watching me—ready to jump me!

Joe swallowed hard and moved on. His eyes darted from side to side so he would not be taken by surprise. He kept his hands up, ready to defend himself, although he wondered what good karate would do against a supernatural assailant! But nothing happened.

Joe was beginning to feel that the scarecrow was not anywhere near when he heard a scratching noise ahead. Something was slinking toward him and jarring the bottom of the cornstalks as it came.

Joe's heart skipped a beat, and his breath came in short gasps. He stopped and waited, preparing to yell for Frank as soon as the scarecrow became visible.

The stealthy sound drew nearer. Joe opened his mouth to shout when a rabbit came bounding through, pursued by a fox. The two animals whizzed past him and disappeared.

He could tell by the noise that they were circling back. The rabbit reappeared. Veering away from Joe, it scooted along a furrow. The fox came in view and, losing the scent, took the opposite direction.

Joe regained his composure and chuckled inwardly at himself. Then he resumed his search.

Frank, meanwhile, was moving gingerly through the cornfield, making sure at each step that he was not trudging into an ambush. He came to a muddy patch where, in the moonlight, he saw footprints leading into a clump where the cornstalks grew closer together. The prints were smudged at the toes.

Frank caught his breath. "The scarecrow!" he muttered. "The upturned toes made the smudges!"

He shifted to one side and sneaked around the spot where the footprints ended. Then, step by step, he silently worked his way toward the spot from the opposite direction. He strained his eyes to see what danger lay ahead of him.

Suddenly he caught the reflection of moonlight on a figure huddled behind the cornstalks. The stovepipe hat was unmistakable. So was the rest of the figure's clothing. It was the scarecrow!

Just then, a twig snapped under Frank's foot. The scarecrow whirled around. Frank's pulse raced, and his throat felt dry.

"Joe! The scarecrow's over here!" he managed to shout.

Before the words were out of his mouth, the apparition leaped to its feet and ran deeper into the field. Frank rushed after it, guiding himself by the racket it made in forcing its way through the cornstalks. The sounds became fainter, but then grew louder again.

It's doubling back, Frank surmised. It's going to jump me. But I'll get it first!

The Walking Scarecrow

Throwing caution to the winds, he advanced quickly in the direction of the noise. A cloud covered the moon just as a figure leaped forward and rushed at him. In the darkness, strong arms clamped themselves around his body. Frank got a headlock on his antagonist and the two fell to the ground, wrestling over and over in a furrow.

They broke free and scrambled to their feet. They were about to continue the struggle when the moon came out again, illuminating both of them.

Frank and Joe Hardy were staring at each other!

"I thought you were the scarecrow!" Joe gasped.

"I thought you were!" Frank panted. "I saw it, but it got away. Well, we might as well go on together, even though I doubt we'll see it again. It must be long gone by now."

The Hardys traversed the cornfield, but their search was fruitless. They made their way back to the center, where the scarecrow's pole was.

The creature was back in its spot!

"I wonder if it'll talk to us this time," Joe said.

"Ask why it's haunting us," Frank suggested.

Joe put the question to the scarecrow. He received no answer.

Frank sighed with exasperation. "Let's return to the house and decide what to do."

They were near the end of the cornfield when a fiery bolt of lightning shot down from the sky. It was so bright that it illuminated the entire area.

With a terrific clap of thunder, the lightning bolt plunged into the old farmhouse. There was a shattering explosion as the roof split apart. Gigantic flames erupted inside the building and roared upward.

Horrified by the spectacle, the Hardys dashed toward the house. But by the time they got there, the structure was a raging inferno. The roof collapsed, the interior beams gave way, and burning planks fell in a heap on the ground floor.

Frank and Joe stopped in the weed-covered driveway. The heat of the fire kept them from going any closer.

"There's nothing we can do," Joe muttered. "The house is gone."

Frank gulped. "It's lucky we weren't inside when the lightning hit! If we hadn't chased the scarecrow, we'd be roasting like hamburgers at a barbecue."

"Well, I suppose this is the end of the old place," a voice suddenly said behind them.

Whirling around, they saw a stranger leaning through the window of a pickup. Neither of the boys had heard him drive up in the noise of the collapsing building. He got out and joined them.

"I'm Josh Compton," the man continued. "I own the farm next door. When I saw the lightning hit the place, I called the fire department, then drove right over. Tell me, who are you?"

The Hardys introduced themselves and explained how their car had broken down on the road.

"We came to the house hoping to phone a garage for a tow," Frank said. "But nobody was here."

Compton shrugged. "Nobody's lived here for twenty years. I keep an eye on the place for a real estate company. But they have not been able to sell it. The fire just may be a blessing in disguise. The house is no great loss, but the land is worth something."

"We were in the house," Joe informed Compton. "We hope it was okay."

"No problem," the farmer assured him. "No reason why you shouldn't use an abandoned house in an emergency."

Frank was mulling over a particular question, which he now put to Josh Compton. "Have you gone into the house lately?"

"Sure. I have a key to the kitchen door. I was over here only yesterday."

"That explains the footprints in the dust," Frank surmised.

Compton chuckled. "I guess so. I never thought about it."

"We also saw some straw in the living room."

"I came directly here from working in the cornfield. The straw must have been on my shoes. By the way, the cornfield belongs to me. My farm is over the hill behind it."

Dawn had broken by now and the house was a mass of cinders. Tongues of flame licked their way through the ruins. A fire truck arrived. Compton described what had happened to the man in charge, then turned back to the Hardys.

"We can't do anything to help. How about coming to my house for breakfast?" he asked.

Joe grinned. "That sounds great!"

Frank nodded. "I'm starved."

The boys followed the farmer to his pickup, and Compton got behind the wheel. "I'll give you a tow to the nearest garage after we've eaten," he offered.

The Hardys accepted gratefully.

"We heard a shout in the cornfield during the night," Frank said on the way to the farmer's home. "We wondered what it was."

"You must have heard me," Compton stated. "I went out to call my dog. He often chases rabbits in the field, and I have to yell my head off to get him to come in again."

"You have quite a scarecrow in that field," Joe said casually.

Compton laughed. "I put it together myself. It's fine except that it doesn't frighten anything, not even the crows!"

Well, it sure gave us a turn, Frank thought. But I better not say it, he'd never believe me!

"The clothes are unusual," Joe went on.

"A joke," Compton admitted. "I found them at an auction, including the shoes with the upturned toes."

They drove on in silence. Frank and Joe reflected on their experience that night and wondered if those events had really happened. Silently they looked at each other, realizing the question had no answer.

At the farmhouse, Mrs. Compton, a friendly, motherly woman, made them feel welcome. She served them a large platter of flapjacks and mugs of cocoa, and talked to them about their hometown of Bayport while they had their breakfast.

When they were finished, they thanked the

woman and Josh drove them to their car, which was still in the ditch where they had left it. He attached a cable to their front bumper and towed the car behind his pickup to a garage about ten miles up the road.

The boys thanked him and offered to pay him for his time and trouble, but he wouldn't hear of it. He accepted their thanks and drove off.

The garage repairman found the problem in the car's fuel pump, which he repaired. Soon the engine purred again and the Hardys were on their way in the direction of the cornfield with Joe at the wheel.

"We'll be passing right by the scarecrow again," he said, "unless it's wandering around the field somewhere."

Frank rubbed the back of his hand across his chin. "Joe, that scarecrow saved our lives," he muttered.

Joe nodded. "It must have known the house would be hit by lightning. That's why it warned us to stay away. When we went in anyway, it lured us out and made us follow it!"

Frank sighed. "But why didn't it simply tell us what would happen?"

"I don't know!" Joe chuckled. "I'm not an expert on scarecrow psychology!"

They reached the point in the road from where they were able to see the weirdly dressed creature. It was on its pole.

"Shall we stop and ask?" Joe suggested, joking.

"Keep going, wise guy!" Frank ordered in the same tone of voice.

They both stared into the cornfield. The scarecrow seemed to smirk knowingly as they passed by.

21

THE MYSTERY OF THE VOODOO GOLD

Frank and Joe Hardy were sauntering along "Underground Atlanta," a collection of shops and stores built below street level.

Joe had bought the latest hit record in a music shop and Frank was carrying a bag from a bookstore.

"It's four o'clock," Frank declared, looking at his watch. "I think we should go back to the hotel and shower. We have a dinner date with Dad at six-thirty, remember?"

Joe nodded when he spotted a strange shop. The front was taken up by a large window decorated all in black. A full-sized skeleton hung in one corner, and there was a display of books about witchcraft, magic, and the occult.

"Hey, Frank!" he exclaimed and pointed. "See that sign over there? It says 'Readings Given.' Let's go in and have our futures told. We have a few minutes to spare."

Frank grinned. "Last time we had our fortunes read was in our sophomore year. The fortune-teller predicted that we both would marry a dark-haired, beautiful girl!"

"It can still happen," Joe said. "Anyway, this might be fun. Let's go in."

The boys entered the store. It was decorated like a witch's cave. Low lighting that changed slowly in color and intensity made everything look spooky, and weird music played in the background.

The walls were lined with cases containing strange merchandise. There were boxes labeled *Love Potion*, *Hate Potion*, and *Career Potion*. There were little open containers with strange, dried-up things, all brown and shriveled. Signs on the containers read *Hair of Dog*, *Eye of Newt*, *Peacock Liver*, *Snake Scales*, and *Mandrake Root*.

"Look at the shrunken heads!" Joe said and pointed to a glass case. "They don't look very friendly."

"If we're not careful, we may wind up right alongside of them," Frank kidded.

"You know," Joe said, "there's something about this place. I can't explain—"

"I know what you mean," Frank said. He was also being drawn into the eerie atmosphere and actually had to remind himself that it was all make-believe.

"I feel as if we're being prepared for a human sacrifice in an Aztec temple," Joe went on, trying to be casual. "Anyway, how come no one is here?"

Just then a sultry voice could be heard from the far end of the room. "And what is your pleasure, gentlemen?"

The boys whirled around and saw a woman emerge from the shadows. She wore a slinky black dress which enveloped her from her throat to her toes. Long black hair covered part of her face, which was pretty in an exotic way. Her dark eyes were somewhat slanted, and green eye shadow and blood-red lips gave her a vampirelike appearance.

"How much does it cost to have a fortune read?" Joe inquired.

"Ten dollars," the woman replied.

Both boys rummaged in their pockets.

"I have four," Frank said.

"I have about seven," Joe offered.

The woman smiled. "Enough for one fortune. Whose shall it be?"

The boys flipped a coin and Frank won.

"Come with me," the woman said and led them through a curtained doorway into another room. This one was even spookier than the shop. It was completely covered in black velvet and lighted by an ultraviolet lamp, so that everyone's teeth and eye-balls glowed ghastly white. Both Hardys had the feeling of being sucked into something they could not escape and hesitated for a moment. But the woman had already sat down at a low table and motioned to Frank to sit next to her. The table was covered with black velvet and on it was a huge crystal ball.

She took the boy's palm and looked at it for a

long time. Joe, who had sat down on a cushion in front of the table, kept staring at her curiously.

"You are eighteen years old," she finally said. "You live in a town near the ocean, in a large white house. You play football and the guitar, and you are a good student. You are also very good at something else—a profession—observing . . . watching. . . ."

She took a piece of paper and a pencil. "Give me the date of your birth," she said.

Frank did and she wrote it down, drawing lines on the paper, crossing the lines, and making a circle.

"Look into the crystal ball!" she suddenly commanded.

Frank obeyed, but he was on his guard. He knew crystal balls were a great way to rivet someone's attention while hypnotizing him, and he felt there was a good chance that that was what the woman had in mind.

But he was wrong. After both had looked into the crystal for about a minute, she became agitated.

"You are a detective!" she cried out angrily. "Why have you come here? I have my license. I am doing nothing wrong. Nothing the police can complain about!"

"I'm not from the police," Frank assured her. "My brother and I are amateur investigators and we came here only to have our fortunes told."

"Oh," she said, obviously relieved. "That is different. I have several private detectives who use my services. You may want to hire me someday. I could be very helpful in some of your cases."

"I bet you could," Frank said. "You know everything about me and you've never seen me before."

"Maybe she's seen our pictures in the paper," Joe offered. "Every once in a while the press writes up our cases."

The woman looked at him, scandalized. "I have never heard of you!" she cried out. "What I told you I knew by intuition. You may not believe me but you will when I'm finished."

She went back to the crystal ball and stared into it once more. "I see motorcycles," she said. "You were both on motorcycles." Her voice became agitated again. "You've done this many times in the past. But now there will be danger. It could be very dangerous!"

"You mean, we'll have an accident?" Frank asked.

"No. It has to do with a new case. I see—I see a man with one blue eye. In a white car. He is very dangerous. Do not listen to him. Stay away from him!"

Her voice was almost a scream now and she appeared to be in a trance, unaware of where she was. Her eyes closed. "Beware of the Green Dragon," she whispered. "Do not go there!"

"What's the Green Dragon?" Joe asked.

But she did not pay attention to him. Her fingernails were digging into Frank's hand, causing him considerable pain.

"Beware of the man with one blue eye!" she panted. "Beware of the Green Dragon. Oh! Oh, I see gold! Much gold, but no good will come of it. Do not touch it. It brings—it brings—death! There is death around this gold and there is—"

Suddenly her eyes opened wide and she stared at Frank with a half-mad look. "Simbu!" she screamed. "Simbu is there! Do not go near him!" She gasped for breath, then she keeled over and fainted on the black velvet floor.

"Quick, Joe, see if you can find a sink and get some water!" Frank urged as he tried to revive the fortune-teller. He rubbed her hands and Joe came a moment later with a soaked hand towel and gently dabbed her forehead.

"For a moment I thought she was putting on an act," Frank murmured. "But she really passed out!"

"What do you think she meant?" Joe was worried.

"If we can revive her, maybe we can ask her," Frank said.

In a few minutes, the woman opened her eyes.

"Are you all right?" Frank asked anxiously.

She nodded slowly. "I received very strong vibrations," she said. "Please, get out of Atlanta as fast as you can!"

"Who's Simbu?" Joe inquired.

"You'll find out if you don't listen to me," she replied. Slowly she got to her feet and walked out into the store. The boys followed. She took a book from a shelf and handed it to Frank. "Here," she said. "If you must know, you can read about him in here. No charge," she added. "My compliments. Now go away and never come back. You are bad luck, gentlemen!"

Frank and Joe stared at her and Frank started to reply, but the expression on her face silenced him. She looked genuinely frightened.

"Come on," he said to his brother and went to the door, nodding good-bye to the fortune-teller.

"Wow!" Joe said when they had left the strange shop. "What an experience!"

Frank nodded. "There was something about her and that place that almost made me believe her."

Joe grinned. "Maybe you should!"

When the boys arrived at the hotel, Frank went to take a shower, and Joe curled up on the bed to read the book the woman had given them. It was about voodoo, the mystical religious cult that flourished on the island of Haiti but had its roots in Africa. The book described the more common practices and spells, incantations, and sacrifices necessary in order to perform various ceremonies.

When Frank came out of the shower, Joe said, "If I wish to cast a spell on you and make your arm hurt, all I have to do is put a needle through the arm of a doll and *you'll* feel the pain."

"Hm, well, don't do it now," Frank said. "We have to meet Dad for dinner, and I don't need a pain anywhere."

"I suppose it wouldn't really work unless you believed in voodoo," Joe went on. "It's all a matter of suggestion."

"Have you found the part on Simbu yet?" Frank asked as he took a clean shirt out of the closet.

"He's a chubby little fellow with rather insane eyes that wander outward," Joe replied. "See, here's a picture of him."

Frank looked over his brother's shoulder at the reproduction. Simbu had both arms up in the air and ten fingers on each hand. He stood with his legs spread apart and had ten toes on each foot. A big belt or girdle encircled his waist.

"Cute," Frank said. "Who's he supposed to be?"

"A rare character who guards his owner's possessions," Joe explained. "Very few Simbu figures from the last century still exist and those that do are very valuable to collectors. There are apparently many modern imitations, but none that could pass as authentic antiques." He handed the book to Frank. "Here, read it yourself while I take a shower."

Frank sat down with the book. It seemed that Simbu was a character who did not want to be collected. His job was to stay by his master's side and protect him from evil. Whenever anyone disturbed Simbu or whatever he was guarding, terrible things would happen.

Two Simbu dolls had been found in Haiti and had been sold to museums. In both cases, the people who had discovered them had died soon thereafter under very mysterious circumstances—and not pleasantly. Not only that, but strange things occurred in the museums. Water pipes burst; heavy plaster fell from ceilings and smashed glass cases; a fire broke out. The problems did not stop until the Simbus were taken back to where they had come from.

Soon Frank and Joe were on their way to the lobby to meet their father. Frank carried a briefcase with several documents for the famous investigator that he had picked up from a law firm in Atlanta.

After they had greeted one another, they went out into the street where Mr. Hardy hailed a taxi.

"Take us to the Green Dragon, please," he told the driver.

"What!" Frank exploded. "Where are we going?"

"A restaurant not far from here," Mr. Hardy said. "I'm sure you'll like it. They have great seafood."

The boys said no more until they were seated at a corner table in the restaurant. Then they told their father about their experience in the afternoon.

"A man with one blue eye, with a white car?" Mr. Hardy mused. "Well, that's no secret. I know who she's talking about."

"You do?" Frank was flabbergasted.

"His name is Pierre Buffon," Mr. Hardy explained. "He wears a white eye patch and drives a white Mercedes. He's one of the most cold-blooded cutthroats in this hemisphere."

"Oh, great," Joe said. "Just the guy we want to meet."

"I've tangled with him several times," Mr. Hardy went on. "But he's a slippery customer. Just when you think you have him nailed, he slips through your net, or the evidence you had evaporates and you're left with nothing while he skips off with the loot. He's a master thief, you see. But I also suspect him of having taken many lives in the course of his work."

"What does he specialize in?" Frank inquired.

"Antiques," his father answered. "Sometimes he holds them for ransom. Other times he sells them to unscrupulous collectors, who are too greedy to care that they can never exhibit them publicly because they would be recognized as stolen goods."

"The fortune-teller mentioned Simbu," Frank said. "He's an antique. It all fits in."

Mr. Hardy nodded. "I know about that deadly little rascal," he said. Then he frowned. "But Buffon is a superstitious person. He'd stay away from anything having to do with a curse."

"It's so crazy," Joe put in. "Do you really believe in that woman's prediction?"

Mr. Hardy shrugged. "Who knows? Perhaps she really sensed something that could happen. We'll find out, I suppose."

"The fact that you took us to the Green Dragon makes me tend to believe in her," Joe sighed. "After all, you knew nothing about what happened this afternoon."

"In that case," Frank said, "my theory is that Buffon got hungry. Maybe he couldn't resist the Simbu despite his superstition."

Joe paid no attention. He stared over his brother's shoulder, his eyes wide with surprise. Frank followed his brother's gaze and almost gasped.

"It's him!" he whispered. "The man with one blue eye!"

Mr. Hardy didn't have to turn his head. Pierre Buffon came right up to their table. "Monsieur Hardy, how pleasant to see you again," he said in an oily, unpleasant voice.

"It's not a pleasure to see you, Buffon," the detective replied. "What do you want?"

"I was occupying this table with some friends

before you came in. One of them dropped an envelope. Nothing important, it has sentimental value only. But he wishes to recover it. Have you seen an envelope, perhaps?"

"No, we haven't," Mr. Hardy said.

"Might I trouble you to stand up?" the man pressed.

Mr. Hardy did not look pleased, but he rose. The boys followed his example. Buffon looked underneath the table and in the seat cushions, but he found nothing. His face was tense. "So sorry to bother you, Monsieur Hardy," he said. "If you should, by any chance, find our letter, please return it. I know I can trust you, because you are an honorable man, yes?" His eyes glittered, and the boys could see that he was furious at having lost an envelope that was apparently very valuable.

Mr. Hardy just shrugged and kept staring at the man.

Buffon's voice became edgy. "I should hate to have to call the police and have them search you and your sons!" He pointed at Frank's briefcase, which stood at the side of his chair.

Mr. Hardy stood up and threw his napkin on the table. "I'm sure that whatever is in that envelope would be very interesting for the police to read. So by all means, call them! We'll wait."

Buffon snarled and mumbled something about the Hardys getting what was coming to them someday. Then he spun on his heel and walked out.

"What do you make of that?" Joe burst out.

"Maybe we should go back and ask the fortune-teller," Frank quipped.

"It is very strange," Mr. Hardy said slowly. "And I have a feeling we haven't seen the last of Buffon yet. Or Simbu."

"Tell us more about Simbu," Frank urged.

"He was known here in the Atlanta region because there's a story dating back to the time before the Civil War that involves one of the dolls," Mr. Hardy began.

"There was a rich old man who lived alone except for a black slave whom he had treated well and who was devoted to him. The slave was a believer in voodoo and eventually converted his master to its practice. They lived in a large house not far from what is now Route three-eighty. A narrow road leads to it from the Cresthaven Diner. Anyway, when the war came and the Union army swept south and east, the old man became worried about his fortune."

"No wonder," Frank said with a grin.

Mr. Hardy nodded. "He converted everything into gold and hid it somewhere in the ground. He left it with nothing to guard it but a Simbu doll made by the faithful slave. The old man and his servant tried to keep the Union army off the property, which is shielded by a stone wall, but they were killed. And as far as we know, no one has ever found the gold."

"What a story!" Joe said. "Hasn't anyone ever looked for the treasure?"

"I suppose so," Mr. Hardy said. "The thing is,

whoever finds it, will also find a valuable Simbu doll."

"Then, would the discoverer fly in the face of experience and take it with the curse attached to it?" asked Frank.

All three fell silent for a while and finished their dinner. Afterward, Frank and Joe took their father to the airport, since he had to go to New York that night.

Frank had an uneasy feeling on the way and looked out the rear window of the taxi. "Someone's following us," he said. At the next traffic light, the car behind them had to pull up close and the boys recognized the one-eyed man's white Mercedes.

"He thinks we have his envelope!" Joe burst out.

"Yes," Mr. Hardy said. "We have to be very careful. You especially, since you're staying here. What are your plans for the next few days?"

"We'll ride up the coast and spend some time at the various beaches," Frank replied. "Oh, by the way, I almost forgot to give you your papers."

He handed Mr. Hardy the documents, and a few minutes later they arrived at the airport. Pierre Buffon was nowhere to be seen. After the detective had boarded his flight, Frank and Joe took another cab to their hotel. Frank spotted Buffon's car across the street.

"I wonder what he's up to," Joe said.

"Maybe he figures we have his envelope and decided to watch our every move," Frank said. "We'll have to keep an eye on him all night."

The boys paid the cabbie and went into the hotel.

When they arrived at their room, Frank tossed his briefcase on the bed. Joe stared at it.

"Frank! Something's sticking to the bottom!" he cried out, pointing. "What is it?"

Frank looked and pulled off an envelope. "I don't believe it!" he exclaimed. "It stuck to my briefcase on a piece of gum! Obviously it's the envelope Buffon was looking for!"

"Open it," Joe urged. "I can't wait to see what has such sentimental value to an arch criminal."

The envelope contained a faded and tattered piece of paper with a strange message written on it. Frank read it aloud:

> Not where you think it be
> But up the hill and down
> The roots sink deep
> And Simbu will not sleep
> If you dare steal the gold
> He will punish you tenfold.

The boys were stunned. "It must be the work of the old man Dad told us about," Joe said finally. "The man who hid the gold with the help of his slave and left a Simbu to guard it."

"Just as the fortune-teller predicted," Frank said, a hollow ring to his voice. "We're being lured to look for the treasure guarded by an idol who brings death to those who fool with it."

"Now who sounds superstitious?" Joe tried to make light of the matter.

"Call it what you want. You have to admit something strange is going on here."

"You're right," Joe said somberly. "What do you think we should do next?"

"Well, I don't think we should just let it go and throw the message in the wastebasket. I'd like to pursue it, and if we find the gold, we can turn it over to the police or some charity to dispose of it."

"That's my feeling too," Joe said enthusiastically.

Frank walked to the window and peered through the curtains to see if Buffon was still watching the hotel. "It's starting to rain," he reported. "And our friend is still out there. Ah! He's pulling away. I suppose he figures we won't go anywhere in a storm."

The skies had opened up and the wind rushed through the treetops.

"Let's fool him!" Joe declared. "It'll be a wet ride, but we have good rain gear and I have a couple of entrenching tools in my luggage that I brought for camping."

"Right!"

A few minutes later, the boys walked out the back door of the hotel to where their bikes were parked. Gently they eased the motorcycles out to the main street, again looking for the white Mercedes. But the coast was clear and the boys accelerated along the mostly empty road to their target, the property near the Cresthaven Diner.

Luck was with them and soon the rain stopped. The clouds cleared away and a beautiful, brilliant moon guided them. They passed the diner and took the road next to it for a few miles. Then they pulled up alongside some heavy road construction equipment that stood near the stone wall enclosing the old man's property. They parked their bikes and walked through the gate. Clouds skittered across the moon. The wind picked up and soon rain started to fall once more.

"This isn't much fun," Joe grumbled, when even the flashlights were of little help in guiding them through wide-spreading oak trees with strands of Spanish moss hanging down from their limbs.

Night birds screamed in their ears and went flapping off in the rain. Frogs were calling. Frank stumbled knee-deep into a swamp and felt something slither across his legs. A snake, or a muskrat? Whatever it was, it scared him out of his wits, and he shot forward as if a jet were attached to him.

"What's the matter with you?" Joe asked.

"Nothing," Frank mumbled. "Except I got attacked by a snake or something."

Joe laughed.

"It's not funny!" Frank grated.

As they got closer to the old house, there was a tremendous crack and a dark tree branch fell straight at Joe. Frank had no time to warn him. Instead, he knocked his brother down with a football block to get him out of the way. The branch was almost a foot in diameter and Joe shivered once he had recovered from his shock.

"That thing could've killed me!" he said hoarsely.

"You want to go back?" Frank asked.

"N-no! There's the house up ahead."

It was not much of a house anymore. The original walls were still there, but the roof was almost gone. Much of the floor had been torn up and the cellar was filled with broken boards and scattered debris.

"Not where you think it be, but up the hill and down," Frank recited from memory, looking around the terrain. It was mostly flat and they already had climbed a little hill to get there.

"Down which way?" Joe asked.

"I suppose we have to go to the back of the house and see what we find."

Behind the building, indeed, the ground sloped down. But to what?

"The roots sink deep, and Simbu will not sleep," Joe intoned. "What roots? I can't even see any big trees anywhere around here."

"Maybe it refers to a root cellar!" Frank said suddenly. "They were common in those days. People stored their vegetables in them before they had refrigeration."

"Good idea," Joe admitted. "Now, where would that root cellar be?"

"We'll have to hop up and down all over that little hill and see if we hear a hollow sound," Frank said. "Come on!"

The boys slipped and slid around in the mud for the better part of an hour when Joe suddenly stopped. "I think I heard a hollow echo around here," he said. "Let's start digging."

For the next half-hour the young detectives kept excavating the dirt until they hit wood. Straining hard, they managed to rip off the half-rotted boards and shone their lights into a dark pit. It was about twelve feet deep and completely empty!

Joe groaned. "All this work for nothing!" he complained.

"Wait a minute," Frank said. "If the old man went to this much trouble, there must be more to it. Maybe the gold was buried under the floor of the root cellar."

The boys hooked up the rope from Joe's tool kit, slid down the twelve feet and began prodding the floor. It didn't take long to find that same hollow sound again. But as they were tearing up the planking over the chamber, the rain began pouring into the root cellar. To make matters worse, the boys found that a groove in the ground that collected water ran down the hill right over the root cellar.

Soon they stood ankle-deep in water and it was climbing.

"We'll probably drown," Joe said darkly. "Maybe we should heed the fortune-teller's warning!"

"You really want to quit now?" Frank asked.

"I suppose not," the younger Hardy replied and tore away another board. Now they could see a small tunnel underneath, less than five feet high. It led up into the side of the hill, away from the flood.

"The old man designed this well," Frank said. "Look, it's nice and dry."

The boys lowered themselves into the tunnel and followed it to a turn about ten feet to the left. Slowly they crawled around the corner, when they suddenly heard a loud *crash!*

A bolt of thunder hit exactly at the moment when they came face-to-face with Simbu. They stared at the little figure that sat atop an iron box. Was the gold inside the box?

"Shall we defy Simbu's curse and look?" Frank whispered.

"I—don't know," Joe breathed.

The more they stared at Simbu's evil little face, the more they hesitated to touch him. At last Frank addressed the ancient guardian. "Simbu, we're not going to hurt you. And we're not going to steal your gold. We just want to see if it's there."

Then he moved the figure and tried to open the box. However, the locks, despite the years underground, were still strong, and they had no tools that could have broken them.

"Now what'll we do?" Joe asked. "We could take Simbu—"

Another terrible crash of thunder interrupted him.

"The water'll build up in the root cellar," Frank warned. "We'd better get out of here. We can always come back tomorrow."

"You're right," Joe said. He was relieved that Simbu and the gold would stay for the time being.

The boys scrambled back down the passageway and hoisted themselves up into the root cellar. With some difficulty they made their way through the rushing water to their rope and climbed out into the raging storm.

"We'd better divert the water from going into the pit or else it'll be a pool in the morning," Frank suggested.

41

Quickly the Hardys dug a shallow ditch around the opening to the root cellar, then replaced the planks, tamped down the earth and sod, and left.

They returned to their bikes and drove to the hotel, where they managed to get into the parking lot without being observed. At least, they did not see Buffon's white Mercedes anywhere.

An hour later, they had an unexpected telephone call from Bayport. Their mother had been taken to the hospital for emergency surgery. Mr. Hardy, who had stopped off in New York, could not be reached for another twenty-four hours, since he was out on Long Island on a stakeout involving boats. So Frank and Joe had to go home fast.

"I suppose we have to postpone our date with Simbu and make arrangements with the hotel to store our bikes," Frank said. "And I'll call the airport right away to book us a flight home."

The following morning, the white Mercedes followed the boys to the airport. "I bet Buffon is real surprised to see us leave," Joe declared.

"I bet he is," Frank agreed. "I hope he doesn't decide to follow us to Bayport, though."

As it turned out, Buffon stayed behind. A month later, Frank and Joe were sitting in front of the fireplace with their friends Tony Prito and Chet Morton, whom they had just told the story.

"So what happened after your mom got out of the hospital?" Chet demanded. "Did you go back to retrieve the gold?"

"We did," Joe said, "but we were too late."

"What do you mean?" Tony asked. "Did someone else get to your friend Simbu first?"

"No. But when we arrived, the highway people had used that heavy construction equipment we had seen that night to build an expressway linking Route three-eighty to an interstate highway. The old man's property had been transformed into six lanes of brand-new concrete!"

THE DISAPPEARANCE OF FLAMING ROCK

Frank and Joe Hardy were driving toward Los Angeles.

"You know," Joe said suddenly to his brother, "we're not far from Flaming Rock."

"Flaming Rock?" Frank asked, puzzled.

"Remember the article we read some time ago about the town that just vanished one day?"

"Oh, yes!" Frank exclaimed. "It was built around a silver mine, in the mountains, a couple of hundred miles from any settled community."

"Right. The mine was discovered during the Civil War and the heyday of Flaming Rock was between 1863 and 1875. Then the town began to disappear in stages."

"I remember," Frank said. "First the people vanished. A prospector, half-mad from hunger and

45

thirst, staggered into Tucson and reported that he had passed through Flaming Rock and found all the people gone."

"It wasn't that they had packed up and moved out in an orderly manner." Joe took up the story. "They left everything behind. Furniture and clothing remained in the houses. Food on stoves was still warm when the prospector arrived. Everything was as it should have been, except there was no sign of life."

"No one paid attention to the prospector's story," Frank said. "They figured he had been driven crazy by the sun and the loneliness. But didn't a reporter eventually go to Flaming Rock?"

"That's right. A newspaper editor sent his son and a group of men to look for the people. They also had terrible luck with the town. They started out rather late in the season and got trapped by early-winter snows. So they had to go home. When they tried again in the spring, they not only failed to find the people of Flaming Rock, they couldn't even find the town!"

"An entire community had vanished from the face of the earth," Frank said.

"Now people began to take the story seriously," Joe went on. "Various theories developed. Indian haters claimed that Flaming Rock had been destroyed by the Indians, and that everyone had been massacred or carried off into captivity. Trouble with that theory was that the Indians in that area had never been involved in much warfare with their white neighbors. Such a ferocious attack followed by the complete destruction of the town was not characteristic of the natives at all."

"I seem to recall that other rumors were circulated," Frank said. "Some people said the plague had struck Flaming Rock and the few survivors had buried the dead, then burned and leveled the town in order to keep the epidemic from spreading."

"Yes, except such an occurrence would have been reported somewhere," Joe said. "Nothing like that happened. "It was also suggested that the people of Flaming Rock were moved away by the government because of some secret project. But no secret project ever came to light."

"The world was left with the mystery of Flaming Rock until the town popped up again in the early years of this century," Frank said. "At that point, two people, unknown to each other, reported stumbling upon it. They told almost identical stories. They had seen the town at night. First they had noticed a light, fairly high in the air, swinging. When they followed it, they found it was in the tower of the Flaming Rock Hotel!"

"Just thinking about that spooky story gives me the chills," Joe said.

Frank nodded. "Remember, when those two guys went into the houses, they discovered everything to be exactly the way the old crazy prospector had described it. Food on the stoves, still warm. Homes that looked like people had left but a few minutes before. But no living creature in sight, not even a dog or a desert scorpion. It was a dead village."

"And then these witnesses disappeared less than

a month later under mysterious circumstances," Joe added. "No one ever has reported seeing Flaming Rock since then."

Frank had slowed the car down. Suddenly both boys looked at each other.

"Are you thinking what I'm thinking?" Frank asked his younger brother.

Joe nodded his blond head and grinned. "You bet! We're not far from the place. Let's check it out!"

The boys turned off the highway onto a feeder road, and after about thirty miles they took a dirt road that climbed straight up into the mountains.

It was a bouncy ride. "This is nothing but a pair of mismatched ruts in the earth," Joe complained. "I bet the last vehicle to travel this way was a Conestoga covered wagon drawn by the strongest oxen in the world!"

Frank chuckled. "Good thing we rented a four-wheel-drive car and have all our camping gear plus plenty of food and water. This is going to be quite an excursion!"

Suddenly Joe groaned. "It's starting to rain!" he exclaimed. "You know what that means. The earth is so dry and packed that it doesn't absorb water easily. Pretty soon we'll have roaring rivers of floodwater coming down these mountains."

He knew from experience that in that part of the world it only rained a few times a year, and when it did, it often turned into a cloudburst that resulted in floods.

Already the boys noticed animals rushing for higher ground. Deer, skunks, and other furry creatures were moving out of the water's path. The road quickly turned into twin streams following the ruts.

The car's windshield wipers were working furiously but could hardly keep up with the drenching downpour. Frank was squinting, trying to see through the sheets of water that pounded them. Suddenly, as they came atop a rocky rise, he stepped on the brakes in surprise.

"Joe! There's a light up ahead!" he cried out.

"It—it's swinging!" Joe said hoarsely. "Just as those people described it."

"And after telling their story, they disappeared and were never heard of again," Frank added. He had stopped the car and the boys stared into the distance.

"Hey, wait a minute!" Joe said. "We don't know what that light up ahead is and whether it's even near Flaming Rock. Let's just keep our wits together, shall we?"

Frank chuckled dryly and accelerated again. "Right."

But soon he jumped on the brakes once more. "Joe—take a look at that sign!" he gulped.

In the beam of the headlights, the boys stared at a battered piece of wood with words carved into it. It read "Flaming Rock, Ariz.—Pop. 434."

"Four hundred and thirty-four men, women, and children, and all of them have disappeared," Joe said.

"Maybe we'll find them," Frank tried to joke. "I wonder what they'd look like after all those years."

"Well," Joe said, "now that we're here we can't back out. Let's investigate the swinging light."

The rain had died down a little and so had the

wind. Frank and Joe took their flashlights out of the glove compartment and left the car. In the drizzle they soon saw the outlines of buildings.

"There it is, the town of Flaming Rock," Frank said as he beamed his light around.

"I see the hotel with the tower," Joe said. "And the light is still swinging."

"We'll have to climb up to see if someone's doing it," Frank said bravely.

The young detectives walked up to the hotel porch and entered the lobby. Without stopping to look around, they took two steps at a time to the second floor and then to the roof. They passed no one on the way.

When they arrived, the lantern swinger, if he had ever existed, was gone. The lantern was there, but the light was out.

Frank touched the glass. "It's still hot!" he cried out.

Chills went down the boys' spines. "Now what?" Joe asked.

"We'll go down again and look for the person who swung this lantern," Frank said with determination. "He or she has to be somewhere."

The Hardys retraced their steps and searched the hotel, calling out as they went. But there was no answer. And just like the prospector who had been there before them, they found everything in place. Clothes hung in some of the rooms. Beds were covered with clean sheets. In the kitchen, food was still cooking and bubbling on stoves with fires burning!

Frank and Joe looked at each other in disbelief.

Too shaken to speak, they walked through the hotel lobby and saw a cigar butt smoldering in an ashtray.

Suddenly they heard a strange noise.

Quack, quack, quack! A child's wind-up toy duck waddled out from under a curtain, walked across the floor, and then fell on its side as it bumped against Joe's shoe.

The boy bent down to pick it up. But he couldn't wind it again because the key was missing. Slowly he set it on the floor again, his hand shaking.

"Frank, there were people here," he whispered. "Living human beings who breathed and laughed and argued were here all around us. Where are they now?"

Frank shrugged helplessly. "Maybe we'll find the answer if we go on searching for it," he declared.

So the boys continued to explore. At the back door, leading into the hotel kitchen, were muddy footprints just like the ones the boys had made when they walked into the lobby.

"Bigfoot was here," Joe said, trying to shake the eerie mood that threatened to stifle them.

"He's supposed to have big feet." Frank grinned. "These are regular size, almost like ours."

The boys went through the rest of the hotel and found more evidence of recent life, but no human being was anywhere to be seen.

Finally they stepped out into the dark again.

Frank beamed his flashlight around. "There are kerosene lamps in front of some of the houses," he noted. "Let's light them. At least we'll be able to see."

"Good idea," Joe said, and the boys proceeded with their task. It proved easy enough since most of the lamps were still full of fuel.

The rain had stopped and a rather sickly looking moon appeared behind a cloud. Yet the erratic desert weather continued to treat the visitors to an occasional lightning flash and a great rumble of thunder, as if to say, "We're not through with you yet, so don't relax!"

The boys approached the church, which was just two doors down from the hotel. It was a simple, rectangular building on top of which the town's carpenters had built a narrow steeple. When the two entered the church, the bell began ringing, sending its ghostly sound vibrating through the night. Terrified, the boys jumped back, and looked at the steeple.

"I don't believe it!" Joe cried out.

"Someone must be pulling the cord!" Frank said. "There's hardly any wind now and it can't move by itself!"

Frank and Joe ran into the church and climbed to the little belfrey. The bell stopped ringing just before they reached it.

Joe pulled the cord. The bell barely moved.

When the boys descended the stairs again, another noise made them jump. A door slammed in the rear.

"It could have b-been the wind," Joe stammered.

"As I said before, there hardly *is* any," Frank pointed out. They continued on to the back door and saw something that chilled them all over again. An arrow was embedded in the wood!

The Disappearance of Flaming Rock

Both boys recalled the legend that Flaming Rock had been wiped out in an Indian attack and stood frozen to the spot.

"Do—do you suppose it's a warning?" Joe muttered.

"But for what?" Frank asked. His practical mind began to rebel against what was happening to them. "I think we may be the victims of a hoax!" he declared. "It's all too pat, too easy. It could be some big, practical joke—maybe a con game pulled by real estate developers. Or perhaps someone's organizing publicity for a TV show. I just don't believe all this is really occurring the way it seems to be."

"I hope you're right," Joe said. "And yet . . ." He did not finish the sentence.

Slowly, the young detectives walked out of the church and down the street. "What shall we check out next?" Joe inquired.

"We'll get done a lot faster if we split up," Frank suggested. "The place is so small that we can holler if we get attacked by anyone."

"Ah, yes." Joe hesitated. "Meet you here in half an hour?"

Frank nodded and walked to the right. Joe took the left, feeling much less brave than his brother, but not wanting to admit it. He went through several houses, finding what seemed to be the usual for Flaming Rock. Fires in the stoves. Food still on tables. Apparently, whatever had happened here had happened at dinnertime, he thought wryly.

Then he came to the schoolhouse. It was the most eerie of all the buildings. There were little desks in neat rows. On top lay open books, inkwells, and quill pens. As the boy gazed around the room, a breeze ruffled some of the pages.

There was chalk and an eraser on the blackboard and the teacher's last message was written on it: "Tuesday, September 23rd. Vocabulary drill." Underneath were the words assigned for that day. One of them was "ghost." Very appropriate, considering what happened to the town, Joe thought.

When he left the school, he passed several more houses and then decided to investigate a bigger building which was the general store. Perhaps something in there would give him a clue as to Flaming Rock's fate!

As he pushed open the door, which squeaked on its hinges, something told him to pull back. But he did not yield to his intuition. The next thing he felt was a hard blow and he crashed to the floor.

Everything went black in front of Joe's eyes. When he came to, his head hurt. He wondered how long he had been unconscious. He sat up and rubbed his forehead. Suddenly he had the feeling that he was not alone in the room.

His heart beat wildly. He felt a bump swelling on the back of his head, covered with something sticky in one spot. Blood, no doubt.

Joe lay back again and closed his eyes. He still sensed another presence. Was it the man who had struck him down? Was his assailant approaching him, ready to finish him off if he showed any signs of life?

Joe was frightened, but finally his curiosity won out. He opened one eye. His flashlight, which he had dropped on the floor, was still on and cast a dim light across the room. Joe's eye swiveled across a row of merchandise stacked neatly along the wall, but with a layer of dust on top. Then he saw him.

He was standing near the great glass candy case. He was an Indian warrior, almost naked except for a loincloth and several strands of beads around his neck. He held a tomahawk in his hand, but it was not raised. Then he began to heft it playfully.

Oh, let this be a dream, Joe moaned inwardly. Please, let it be a dream!

The Indian was dark and had a strong and handsome face. Around his forehead he wore a headband studded with turquoise. Actually, he was a grand sight. But Joe was too frightened to realize that there was nothing hostile in the man's expression.

He stared at the loosely held tomahawk in the Indian's hand and kept silently praying that the brave would put it down far away from him. He also tried to convince himself that the Indian was nothing but a symptom of his own overactive imagination.

Just then the Indian began to speak. His voice was very deep and controlled, yet there was something ghostly about it.

"You are trespassing on sacred ground!" the apparition intoned. "Ever since the land was stolen, it has been cursed for as long as the grass grows. Because of the atrocities committed against my tribe by the drunken miners, the people of Flaming Rock are doomed to wander, homeless, for all eternity!"

Joe sat up and stared at the man, who seemed real

and unreal at the same time. "Wh-what happened?" he managed to mumble.

The Indian paid no attention to his question, but went on in the same, even tone.

"You and your brother will be spared. But only if you go back and tell what you have seen. Now, leave this place at once!"

Joe shivered. If you only knew how much I want to leave, he thought. But he said nothing.

The Indian took off his headband and folded it up carefully. Then he stepped forward and placed it on the counter.

"Take this!" he said. Then, suddenly, he was gone.

Joe sat, too stunned to move. I wonder where Frank is, he thought dully. Why isn't he here when I need him? Suddenly it occurred to him that his brother might be needing him even more. He may be in worse shape than I, Joe figured and stood up. His limbs still ached from his fall, but apparently he was not injured seriously.

Gingerly he touched his bruise again, relieved that he felt no nausea, which might have indicated a concussion or a fractured skull.

He still wondered if the Indian had socked him with the tomahawk. No, he finally decided. That would have cracked my head for sure. Those things are deadly weapons!

He picked up his flashlight. On the floor, he noticed an old-fashioned coal scuttle turned on its side. It was a peculiarly shaped pail in which people used to carry the coal they burned in their fireplaces and stoves.

Joe beamed his light around. At least a dozen such coal scuttles were hanging over the door, and he saw that one of them had simply fallen from its nail. "That's what clouted me!" he cried out aloud. "It wasn't the Indian at all, just another of those weird accidents that make it such fun to walk around Flaming Rock!"

Then he stepped to the counter. The headband was still there. He reached out and took it. It felt real. Joe stared at it for a moment, then put it in his pocket. Finally he went out of the general store.

He stumbled a little, still dizzy from his ordeal, and tried to breathe deeply in the cool night air. His head pounded with pain. He called out for his brother, but his voice sounded weak, and there was no reply.

He called again and felt even dizzier. He started to hallucinate and imagined seeing eyes glowing in the dark and hearing people talking, shuffling, walking around him.

He shook his head, trying to clear the cobwebs. Then he realized there were desert animals and other nocturnal creatures around, trying to find acorns or other food. Strange, Joe thought. Earlier there had been no sign of life at all, now I see squirrels and mice. And they were real, he knew.

He moved on again, and went through the house next to the general store. He beamed his light around, but found nothing unusual. Afterward he called his brother again, but received no reply. I just have to keep looking in all the houses, Joe thought. I hope I'll find him!

The next place had a cellar with two big doors opening out from it. Joe decided to explore it. He opened the doors with some difficulty. They were very heavy and the hinges had rusted. The basement was filled with tools, old pieces of timber, and some broken furniture. Joe walked inside. Suddenly he froze. He realized that he had stepped right over a snake that was just as surprised as he.

Now it coiled between him and the door, and he could see in the beam of his light that it was a diamondback rattler!

Joe had no doubt that the snake was real. He stood stock-still, beads of perspiration breaking out on his forehead. Then he heard a noise. A little pack rat, who apparently had been sharing this part of the cellar with the rattler and had managed to survive, appeared off to one side, staring at both Joe and the snake. Then it jumped straight up in the air and ran for the corner. The rattler struck instinctively in that direction, but missed by a good foot.

But the strike had carried it far enough away from the door so Joe could jump past it and rush out of the basement.

Frank, meanwhile, had been exploring several homes and had arrived at the town jail. It consisted of a waiting room/office and two cells. Frank beamed his light along the walls and found that things were written on them.

"Graffiti, 1870 style!" the boy exclaimed.

The Disappearance of Flaming Rock

Most of it were drawings and Indian words. Frank chuckled to himself. Probably curses called down on the heads of white men, he thought. He assumed that the jail had been used mainly to house Indians, whom the white men had at first made drunk with cheap whiskey and then had cheated out of their property before imprisoning them until they sobered up.

He wandered inside the first cell. Suddenly he heard the door click behind him. He whirled around and tried to push it open, but it would not budge. He was locked in!

Yet there was not a soul in sight, and not even the slightest breeze was blowing. Who had shut the door?

A chill went down Frank's spine. "Joe!" he cried out as loudly as he could. "Joe, help!"

But his brother did not answer. He's probably at the other end of town, doing his own exploring, Frank reasoned. I just hope *he* doesn't get trapped anywhere! The thought frightened him even more. Would the Hardys be locked up forever in a town that didn't even exist?

Joe, meanwhile, was making his way closer to the prison, and every time he finished investigating another building, he called out for his brother. Finally he heard a faint reply.

"Here, Joe! I'm in jail!"

Joe rushed toward the low structure as fast as he could and dashed inside. When he saw Frank's face behind the bars, he couldn't help but laugh.

"It's not funny!" Frank grated. "Now, let me out,

will you? I noticed a key on the wall right over your head."

Joe took the key from a nail and put it in the door. But it would not turn! He pushed the door open. "It wasn't locked, dummy!" he declared.

Frank stared at him. "It was a minute ago. Don't you think I tried to get out?"

"How'd you get in?"

"I just walked in and the door shut behind me. There was no one around and no wind. Don't ask me how it happened."

"I believe anything," Joe murmured.

"Look at the stuff on the walls," Frank said. "Some of it I can't decipher, but the drawings are interesting."

"I'm not coming into that cell!" Joe protested. "What if the door locks when we're both inside?"

"You're right," Frank said. "Anyway, there's more in the waiting room." He walked out of the cell and the boys beamed their lights into every corner. Suddenly Joe stopped and started to read an inscription.

"Hey, Frank, listen to this! It says 'On this day, in the white man's calendar March 6, 1871, six Indian braves were hanged for stealing horses they did not steal. Tomorrow, the rest of us go to join our brothers on the white man's gallows. Flaming Rock and all its people will be cursed for this crime. The Great Spirit will sweep down and take them from the good land, the land they ripped open with their mines and laid to waste with their carelessness. The Great Spirit will make Flaming Rock a hole in space. No more.' "

"Fantastic!" Frank exclaimed. Quickly he pulled a pencil and a piece of paper out of his pocket and copied the inscription.

"Do you think that's what happened?" he asked when he was finished.

"I was told the same thing by an Indian brave a little while ago," Joe said.

"You what?"

"You heard me. I went into the general store, got conked out by a coal scuttle, and when I came to this guy stood there with a tomahawk in his hand. He told me the town had been doomed because of what they did to his tribe, but that you and I would be spared if we left right away and told what we saw."

"How—how do you know you weren't just seeing a ghost?" Frank asked.

"He may have been a ghost, but he had a real headband on." Joe pulled the gift out of his pocket. "Here. He gave it to me."

Frank fingered the headband in awe. "This is incredible!" he said finally. "Joe, what do you think we should do?"

"Leave," Joe said simply.

"Maybe one of us should stay and wait for the other to bring the sheriff in the morning?"

"I don't think so," Joe said. "By morning the town may be gone, and whoever stays right along with it!"

Frank nodded glumly. Then he brightened. "I tell you what. Why don't we return to the car and spend the night? If the town's still here in daylight, we'll take pictures. At least we'll have some proof that Flaming Rock really existed."

"Great! I'll go along with that," Joe said. "And now, let's hurry away from here. This place gives me the creeps!"

The boys went back to their car and managed to catnap fitfully through the night. When the sun rose in the morning, they quite expected the village to have disappeared. But to their surprise, it was still there!

Frank took his 35mm camera from the glove compartment and shot almost a whole roll of film of the mysterious place. With the help of a telephoto lens, he got close-up pictures of the hotel, the store, the schoolhouse, and the jail.

"This should do it," he said with satisfaction when he had snapped the last frame. "Now people will *have* to believe us."

Joe was less confident. "The story has been told before, and the people who told it have vanished," he said gloomily.

"Your Indian friend asked you to report what you saw," Frank reminded him. "And I have a feeling he was a good sort. He'll watch over us."

"I hope so," Joe said and started the car.

They carefully drove back down the same rutted road they had taken the day before. When they got to the top of a rise, Frank turned to take one last look at Flaming Rock.

"Joe!" he cried hoarsely. "It's gone!"

"What?" Joe jumped on the brakes and, when the

car had stopped, turned around. The town was no longer there.

"Spooky!" Chet Morton declared when he heard the story a few days later. "Did you show the pictures to the closest police chief out there?"

"There were no pictures," Frank said.

"What do you mean? You took them, didn't you?"

"Yes. But not a single one turned out. All were fogged."

Biff Hooper, who sat next to Chet on the sofa, nodded. "Of course they didn't turn out, because the whole thing never really happened," he declared. "It was something like autosuggestion on the Hardys' part. They were set off by the magazine article they read and imagined the whole thing."

"What about this?" Joe pulled out the headband and handed it to his friend.

"It looks new," Biff stated. "No more than a few years old."

"That's true," Joe admitted. "But there are some Apache markings on the inside. I had an Indian friend translate them for me. It's the name of a chief who was killed by miners on March sixth in Flaming Rock."

"But this is ink," Chet said, after he had studied the headband closely. "As far as I know, the Indians didn't write with ink."

"Right," Biff added. "You were duped, you see?"

"No, we weren't," Joe replied. "The Indians did use white man's ink after trade had been established.

And here's the kicker. The chemist said that this ink, though it looks new, tested out to be of a kind that hasn't been manufactured since 1880!"

This convinced Chet. His face became worried. "What did you say happened to those guys who went to Flaming Rock before you?"

"We don't know. They disappeared," Joe replied.

Chet sighed. Then he stood up and went to the telephone. "What are you doing?" Frank inquired.

"I'm going to call all our friends. From now on, you two won't go anywhere without a bodyguard!"

THE
PHANTOM
SHIP

Frank and Joe were out in their motorboat, the *Sleuth*. Frank shaded his eyes with his hand and gazed around at the surging waves dotted with whitecaps.

"Looks like a storm coming up, Joe," he said to his brother. "We'd better get out of the Atlantic before it gets any worse."

Joe wiped drifting spray from his face. "It's getting dark," he noted. "But we're not far from the bay. Let's head home. I'll rev up the motor and gain some speed."

The Hardys often took their boat out into the Atlantic, but when a storm began on the ocean, they knew they had to get back into Barmet Bay, which was near their home in Bayport, for safety. Otherwise, the *Sleuth* might sink or overturn.

65

Joe pressed the accelerator. The boat shot forward in a burst of speed. But suddenly the engine sputtered, then stopped, and they came to a halt in the water. Joe struggled to get the boat started again, but in vain.

"No use," he said at last. "It's conked out." The brothers checked every part of the mechanism according to the manual. When they had finished, Frank scratched his head.

"Everything seems just fine, Joe. Transmission, oil, gas—everything."

"But the engine won't start," Joe declared.

"Well, we'd better get help. It's a long swim from here to the bay!"

Frank took the transmitter of the ship-to-shore radio and flipped the switch. Nothing happened! He levered the switch up and down, examined the cord, and checked the batteries.

"Nothing wrong with the radio," he muttered, "except the fact that it won't work, either. It's odd. We must be under a hex or something."

The *Sleuth* rocked helplessly in the waves churned up by strong winds as darkness fell. There was no moon, and black clouds covered the stars. Frank and Joe shivered in the cold.

"Looks like we'll have to spend the night out here," Joe mumbled. "I just hope we don't capsize!"

"We don't have much chance of being picked up, either," Frank said glumly. "I can hardly see my hand in front of my face. Even if a ship came past, they'd never spot us."

Suddenly a towering black mass loomed toward

them in the darkness. A harsh voice shouted over the water: "Who are you?"

"It's a ship!" Joe exclaimed exultantly. "And someone saw us!" He cupped his hands around his mouth and shouted back, "We're Frank and Joe Hardy! We're marooned! Can you take us aboard?"

"Aye, we can do that!" came the reply.

The black mass moved closer and stopped beside the *Sleuth*. A lantern swaying in the wind revealed the curving bow of a large ship. On the bow were painted in white letters the words *Samoa Queen*.

A rope ladder fell down the side of the vessel until it dangled over the *Sleuth*. Frank gripped the ropes on either side, got his foot onto the bottom rung, and quickly climbed up. Joe tied the launch to the ladder and followed.

The Hardys vaulted over the railing and came down on a deck of massive oak planks. In the dim light of old-fashioned lanterns they saw they were on a sailboat. The sails billowed in the wind and the mainmast pointed high into the dark sky. A flight of wooden steps led up to the wheelhouse.

A crew of rough-looking sailors were on deck. They wore old-fashioned work clothes and stood silently, glowering at the newcomers. One held a harpoon in his hand and waved it menacingly.

"This must be some sort of training ship," Frank said to Joe in a low tone.

"Well, it's the spookiest training ship I've ever seen," his brother whispered back.

A man in a salty pea jacket strode toward them. He was tall and gaunt with a black beard and piercing black eyes. When he spoke, they recognized the harsh voice that had hailed them over the water.

"So you are Frank and Joe Hardy, are you?" he growled. "Those names mean nothing on my ship!"

Joe spoke up boldly. "Who are you?"

"Captain Jonathan Parker. The *Samoa Queen* is a whaler from Nantucket. And I need more able-bodied seamen for a voyage to the Pacific. You two will do. You will be members of my crew until we get back to Nantucket."

Frank and Joe stared at one another in the murky light of the ship's lanterns. They were thinking the same thing. Sailing ships had not made whaling voyages since the nineteenth century!

He must be kidding, Joe thought. Aloud he said, "Captain Parker, there's no reason for us to stay aboard the *Samoa Queen*. All we need is help with our engine."

" 'Engine'? What is an 'engine'?" Parker snarled.

That's got to be a joke, Frank told himself. To the captain he said, "Well, you need power to drive a ship, don't you?"

"Aye. The power of wind and sail!" Parker thundered. "What other kind of power is there to drive a ship across the ocean? Or maybe you paddle across!"

The sailors behind him burst into wild laughter. Parker joined in the laughter, which rose to a high-pitched cackle in the moaning of the wind across the deck.

"These guys are weirdos!" Frank exploded. "Let's go back over the side—we'll be better off drifting in the *Sleuth*!"

The Phantom Ship

The Hardys ran to the railing where they had climbed up the rope ladder. But when they peered down, they froze. The *Sleuth* was gone!

"Grab them!" Parker ordered his crew.

The sailors rushed forward and seized Frank and Joe, who were forced back into the middle of the deck. Captain Parker confronted them furiously.

"I know your game," he rasped. "You want to sign on another whaler. Well, it is too late. You will stay aboard the *Samoa Queen*. We are headed around Cape Horn into the Pacific, and on our trip I will make whalers of you or throw you to the sharks!"

The Hardys felt cold chills as they listened to Parker's tirade. To Frank it seemed as if they had fallen into the hands of lunatics. Joe wondered if they were living a nightmare.

Abruptly Parker turned toward the wheelhouse, and yelled, "Amos Langton, come down here!"

A burly sailor emerged and descended the steps to the deck. Parker ordered him to take the Hardys below and get them ready for sea duty. Langton led the boys across the heaving ship. Behind them, they heard the eerie laughter of the captain and his strange crew.

"I am the first mate," Langton said as they went down the stairs. "I will show you where you will stay when you are off duty."

"But what's this all about?" Joe inquired.

"You know very well what this is about," the first mate reproached him sternly.

"No, we don't!" Frank protested.

Langton turned and confronted them at the bottom of the stairs. "Then you had better learn fast. Follow orders, always! Sailors who disobey orders on this ship get thrown to the sharks!"

The Hardys shuddered as they remembered Captain Parker's threat.

Langton took them into the living quarters of the crew. They saw a large, spare room with bunks along the walls. Beneath each bunk hung a harpoon, and next to it were oilskins to be worn over pea jackets and a sou'wester for use as a hat during bad weather.

"Take those two empty bunks and get ready for duty on deck," the first mate ordered. Then he turned and left.

The ship began to move, forcing Frank and Joe to shift their feet to keep their balance. The timbers creaked and swayed from side to side. A lantern on a chain overhead threw a flickering light across the room. It gave off a greasy smell.

"That's whale oil," Joe said.

Frank nodded. The brothers had experimented with all kinds of fuel in their detective work, and recognized whale oil as easily as wood smoke.

"Trouble is," Frank went on, "that stuff went out when kerosene came in. What's happening here?"

"I have no idea," Joe replied. "But we'd better be careful until we find out."

He called a greeting to the sailors who were lounging in several of the bunks.

They stared at him somberly without answering.

"We're new here," Joe went on in a friendly tone.

The men still said nothing.

"They're a cheerful lot!" the boy muttered. "Silent as the grave."

"And what about this ship?" Frank said. "It's a phantom, just like these guys!"

"I hope we don't have to sail on the *Samoa Queen* forever," Joe said with a shudder.

Near them, an evil-looking sailor was working on his harpoon. He polished the wooden shaft and oiled the long steel blade. Then he took a file and sharpened the point, which had a tong curving backward like that of an enormous fish hook.

Joe decided to make conversation. "That looks like a dangerous weapon," he observed.

"Dangerous to whales, or my name is not John Corkin!" the man snapped. "And dangerous to landlubbers who think they are whalers!"

Corkin was so hostile that Joe made no reply.

Frank turned to the sailor on the other side, a grizzled veteran who looked friendlier. "What's your name?"

"Orne. I come from New Bedford. We are an old whaling family, we are."

Encouraged by Orne's amiable demeanor, Frank continued the conversation. "What's the real story of the *Samoa Queen*?"

Orne looked surprised. "Why, she is a whaling ship from Nantucket."

"Where's she bound?"

"Around Cape Horn. If you do not know that, why did you sign aboard?"

Before Frank could reply, Joe intervened. "Whaling voyages around the Horn go back to the nineteenth century," he insisted.

Orne looked puzzled. "Right you are, mate," he said, "and this is the year 1850!"

The Hardys were startled by the statement. Corkin, who had been listening, spoke sarcastically. "You two must be stupid if you do not know what year it is!" He laughed loudly.

The other sailors except Orne joined in one by one until a mad cackle echoed through the ship like a chorus of witches.

The Hardys were horrified by the grinning faces and weird laughter. They leaped to their feet.

"We know what time it is!" Joe exploded. "It's time for us to jump ship!"

Frank supported Joe wholeheartedly. "You can have the *Samoa Queen* and the whales!"

Corkin glared savagely. Raising his harpoon, he hurled it at them.

Frank and Joe ducked as the sharp weapon zoomed through the air over their heads and slammed into one of the ship's timbers. The harpoon hung there, quivering under the rise and fall of the waves.

"That was a close call!" Joe gulped.

"Get ready," Frank warned. "Here they come!"

Led by Corkin, the sailors rushed at the boys, who went into a protective karate stance and prepared to defend themselves. The crowd of grinning faces pressed in on them and a multitude of hands reached out.

The Phantom Ship

Just then a shout came from the deck. "Thar she blows! Off the starboard bow!"

Langton appeared in the doorway. "The lookout sighted a whale!" he shouted. "Frank and Joe Hardy, up on deck! And bring your harpoons!"

The men who had threatened the boys retreated sullenly. Frank and Joe walked through their ranks, reached the door, and hurried upstairs.

It was still dark, but the sea was calmer and the ship moved slowly across choppy waves.

With Captain Parker giving orders, a dozen men were getting a whaling boat ready for action. They lifted the vessel from its stanchions by means of chains and pulleys, and swung it over the side, where it hung suspended in the air.

As the Hardys watched, Frank wondered aloud, "How can there be whaling off Barmet Bay?"

Captain Parker heard him. "Barmet Bay?" he roared. "We have rounded Cape Horn and are now in the Pacific!"

Impulsively Joe asked, "How could we reach Cape Horn in one night? Even a nuclear-powered aircraft carrier couldn't move that fast!"

"What is an 'aircraft carrier'?" Parker demanded suspiciously. "And what does 'nuclear' mean?"

Joe shrugged. "Nobody will know for a hundred years."

"What are you talking about?"

"The twentieth century!"

"You must be crazy," Parker muttered. "You make no sense."

Frank nudged Joe with his elbow, as if to say, "Easy! We don't need any more trouble!"

By now the whaleboat was ready to be manned. Sailors clambered in and took their places at the oars on either side. Langton stepped in amidships.

"Frank Hardy, you will be the harpooner. Get in the bow," the first mate said. "Joe Hardy, you will steer the boat, so you get in the stern behind the tiller."

When the boys were aboard, the men on the pulleys lowered the whaleboat into the water, and the oarsmen pulled away from the Samoa Queen. Joe followed Langton's orders and worked the tiller back and forth to keep on course. Frank braced himself in the bow with the harpoon in his hand.

"There is the whale's waterspout!" Langton cried. "Joe Hardy, veer to the left!"

Joe moved the tiller. "I don't see anything over there," he declared.

"Then you are no whaler! Follow my orders or you will walk the plank!"

The boat continued to the left over the dark water. A single star peeped through the murky clouds overhead. The oars rose and fell rhythmically.

"This is the place," Langton declared. "Frank Hardy, throw your harpoon!"

Frank shook his head. "There's no whale here!" he protested.

"Yes, there is! Throw your harpoon!" the first mate bawled at him.

The Phantom Ship

Frank hurled his harpoon deep into the water. Then he drew it in by the rope attached to it. Secretly, he was glad he hit nothing.

Langton shook with fury. "You lost the whale! You let him get away!"

Joe came to Frank's support. "I didn't see any whale, either."

"Then you steered the wrong way!" Langton shouted. "I will report you both to Captain Parker when we get back to the *Samoa Queen*. Circle the area. Maybe I will spot the whale again. And this time, Frank Hardy, you had better catch him!"

Joe shifted the tiller and the oarsmen strained at the oars. Frank kept scanning the water in the bow. The boat moved around and around.

Seeing no sign of the whale, Langton finally gave up and ordered a return to the *Samoa Queen*. The whaleboat was lifted aboard and replaced on its stanchions.

"We lost the whale!" the first mate reported to the captain. "The Hardys were responsible."

Parker was infuriated. "Lock them up!" he commanded.

The boys were pushed downstairs and put into a barred cell used as the ship's prison. Then the door banged shut and they were left alone. A whale-oil lantern illuminated two wooden bunks and a small table in the middle of the room. The brothers sat down and looked at each other.

"This is getting weirder and weirder," Joe said. "We're on a phantom ship, being held prisoner by a crew of ghosts!"

"Done in by a ghost whale," Frank added morosely.

Joe pinched his lower lip. "Yet Langton said he saw the whale."

"It's his word against ours, Joe, and you know who Parker will believe. Besides, Langton's a ghost himself! Why couldn't he see a whale that isn't there?"

"What do you think they'll do with us?" Joe asked.

Frank shrugged and the Hardys fell silent. Both were thinking about Parker's threat to feed them to the sharks.

"Are there such things as ghost sharks?" Joe went on. "The kind that don't really eat you?"

"Let's hope so," Frank replied.

A sound on the stairs interrupted them. They jumped up and listened as footsteps came toward them. Only one man was approaching, so the boys stepped into the middle of the room and waited to see what would happen.

Corkin appeared, carrying a harpoon in his right hand.

"So you lost the whale," he sneered at them. "You do not know how to steer a boat or how to harpoon a fish. I should have been there. No whale ever gets away from me!"

Frank chuckled. "I believe you're jealous because I went along as a harpooner instead of you," he said.

Corkin raised his weapon and hurled it between the bars. It was aimed directly at Joe, who did not have time to dodge out of the way.

But Frank had anticipated the attack. He tipped the table up in the air in front of his brother. The harpoon plunged into the top and pierced the wood. Its sharp point came right through on the other side, only inches from Joe! He wiped a trickle of sweat from his face as Frank wrenched the harpoon from the table.

"Corkin, that's the second time you've thrown this thing at us. Now it's your turn to be on the wrong end!" the older Hardy cried. He lifted the weapon and rushed forward. Corkin turned pale, backed away, and fled up the stairs to the deck.

Frank tossed the harpoon into a corner of the cell and laughed. "I wasn't really going to spear him, just wanted to scare him off. Anyway, he doesn't have his toy anymore. I wonder how he'll explain that to the first mate the next time they go after a whale!"

Suddenly another footfall could be heard on the stairs.

"Probably Corkin again," Joe said apprehensively. "Maybe he's coming for another round with us."

"Well, we'll be ready this time," Frank vowed and retrieved the harpoon. He held it up defensively, but a moment later he lowered it as he realized the newcomer was Orne.

The sailor shuffled toward the bars, all the while glancing over his shoulder. "I should not be here, mates," he whispered. "I am on duty up top. But there is something I wanted to tell you."

"What is it?" Joe inquired.

"Captain Parker has it in for you. He is keeping

77

you locked up because he may need you before the voyage is over. But he will throw you to the sharks before we return to Nantucket."

"We'd better get out of here," Frank said. "Can't you help us?"

"All we want is a fighting chance to save ourselves," Joe added.

Orne shook his head. "I am just an ordinary deckhand. There is no way I can release you. It would do no good, either. We are in the middle of the ocean. What would you do? Swim a thousand miles to land?"

Joe became excited. "Perhaps we could launch a whaleboat and get away."

Orne shook his head again. "There is always someone watching the deck from the wheelhouse. You would be spotted. Besides, it takes more than two to launch a whaleboat. Now that you know what to expect, I would like you to tell me something."

"Sure," Joe said. "After all, you took a chance coming down here and warning us."

"Why do you talk so strangely?" Orne wanted to know. "Here it is 1850, and you mention the twentieth century and power other than sails. Are you clairvoyant?"

The boys exchanged baffled glances. How could they make him understand?

"We can't tell him we think he's a ghost," Joe murmured to Frank.

"It's a question of time," Frank replied loudly to the man's question. "We cannot tell what time it is. By centuries, anyway."

Orne pointed to a calendar on the wall. The numbers 1850 were written on it in large letters.

"I guess that has to be the year as long as we're aboard ship," Joe commented.

Orne frowned. "You two have not escaped from an asylum, have you?" he asked anxiously.

"No, we haven't," Frank assured him. "But we'd sure like to escape from this ship!"

Orne nodded. "I will help you later if I can. Now I have to get back on duty." The sailor vanished up the stairs.

Frank lay down on his bunk with his hands behind his head. Joe sat on the table with his legs dangling over the edge. They discussed their predicament, using their detective training to analyze the facts.

"The trouble is," Frank observed, "we can't figure out what to do since we're dealing with phantoms. They kidnapped us, but how do you outwit somebody who lived in 1850?"

Joe scratched his head. "We'll have to play it by ear, Frank. I tell you what. If Captain Parker lets us out of here, let's show him we're good sailors. If we're handy enough around the ship, maybe he'll change his mind about dumping us overboard."

"Good thinking. It may be our only chance. But you know something," Frank added, glancing at his wristwatch. "It's only a few hours since we were picked up from the *Sleuth*. How can all these things have happened to us?"

Joe was about to say something when an odd

feeling made him turn his head. He was startled to see a man in sailor's garb at the door to their cell. Struck by Joe's amazed expression, Frank raised his head and looked in the same direction.

The man stood, silently gazing at them. He was a ghostly figure with a gleaming white face and long, tapering white fingers clutching one of the bars. His face had no expression, and his blue eyes were fixed on them.

"How did he get here?" Joe mumbled. "I didn't hear him come down the stairs."

Frank sat up. "Neither did I. He doesn't look like one of the crew."

Suddenly the weird stranger beckoned to them to follow him.

"Who are you?" Frank demanded. "And why should we go with you?"

"It's impossible, anyhow," Joe pointed out. "The first mate locked the door when they threw us in here. Unless you have a key?"

To their astonishment, the man pulled the door open. He gestured at them again by crooking his finger.

"He doesn't need a key!" Joe gulped.

"We might as well go with him," Frank advised. "Maybe he'll show us how to escape from this tub. But he could be dangerous, too, so watch out."

Joe nodded and the Hardys stepped out of the cell. Their eerie guide closed the door silently, then walked to the stairs and started up. His feet made no sound as he ascended to the deck.

The Phantom Ship

The uncanny silence unnerved the Hardys. Joe got goose bumps, and Frank felt a cold chill run down his spine.

At the top of the stairs, the man stepped out on deck and started toward the stern of the ship. Frank and Joe stopped at the doorway and cautiously peered through to see if anyone was there. But the whale-oil lantern flickering in the darkness told them the deck was empty.

Their silent guide turned and once more beckoned to them. Obediently, they followed him across the deck.

They felt the up-and-down sweep of the stern as it rose and fell under the surge of great waves. Looking down, they saw the water churning into a bubbling white froth. Out of the black, starless sky came the harsh scream of a seabird.

The uncanny stranger stopped and stared at the Hardys with eyes that never blinked.

What's he going to do now? Frank asked himself. Will he try to push us overboard?

Suddenly the man pointed into the darkness directly astern. Straining their eyes, the Hardys were able to make out the bow of a ship! It was following the *Samoa Queen!*

The mysterious sailor pointed down into the water and then at the bow of the ship.

Joe was galvanized. "He's telling us to swim to that ship! It's near enough, so let's go!" He mounted the rail and prepared to dive into the ocean.

Frank took Joe by the elbow. "Wait a minute. Let's make sure that that's really what he means."

They turned to face their strange escort once more, but the man had vanished! Speechless, the boys looked over the stern again. The ship was gone, too!

The Hardys were thunderstruck. Joe climbed down from the rail.

"Are we seeing things?" he asked. "Are we suffering from hallucinations?"

"I don't know," Frank replied.

A voice suddenly spoke behind them. "Mates, you are taking a big chance!"

They whirled around. Orne stood there, his face worried. "I was on duty in the wheelhouse," he explained. "That is how I saw you come on deck. I do not know how you escaped from the jail, but if you get caught, you will have a long swim home!"

Joe was perplexed. "Did you see where that other sailor went?" he inquired.

"What other sailor? You two are alone. There is no one else on deck with you and no one was here before."

"What about the ship following the *Samoa Queen*?" Frank asked.

Orne looked at them as if they were insane. "There is no other ship. Now, go back below and rest. Langton will be coming on inspection anytime now. He better not see you up top!"

Orne left and the Hardys quickly made their way back to their cell. The door swung open when Frank pulled it, but when he let it close behind them, it locked itself!

"Even the door's jinxed," he muttered.

The Phantom Ship

The boys lay down on their bunks trying to sort out the weird events they had just been through.

Joe was the first to speak. "That sailor must have been an apparition among ghosts!"

Frank shuddered. "A phantom on a phantom ship. It's crazy."

At that moment a terrific clap of thunder sounded overhead. The ship began to pitch and toss. Shouting could be heard on deck.

Then Langton appeared below. "We are in a storm!" the first mate shouted. "We need every hand on deck!" He unlocked the door and gave the Hardys their orders. "Put on your foul-weather gear and get up top!"

He raced off, and Frank and Joe ran to the sleeping quarters. They donned their oilskins, sou'westers, and rubber boots, then went upstairs.

The sky was black and angry. Rain fell in torrents. A twisting wind created mountainous waves, causing the *Samoa Queen* to bob like a cork in a rushing river. Waves broke over the bow and sloshed across the deck.

Captain Parker cupped his hands around his mouth and bawled orders into the raging storm. Some of the men responded by furling the sails so they wouldn't catch the wind, while others battened down the hatches to prevent water from spilling in. Several crew members fought their way along the rails hand over hand to get from the bow of the ship to the stern.

Langton came up from inspecting the hold. "We have sprung a leak!" he shouted.

"Take Frank and Joe Hardy and plug it," Parker yelled back.

The boys went with the first mate. In the hold, they saw a split timber, allowing water to seep in from outside. A couple of inches had already collected on the floor.

"Frank Hardy, get the pump from the locker and pump the water into that barrel in the corner," Langton commanded. "Joe Hardy, help me plug the leak!"

He produced a box of tools and a flat board that he held in place over the leak. Joe took a hammer from the box and began driving nails into the board. He worked rapidly and expertly, hitting the nails on the head with every swing of the hammer.

When he finished, the board held the two sides of the split timber together, and the water stopped coming into the hold.

"Good!" Langton complimented Joe.

Meanwhile, Frank had removed the pump from the hold locker. It was a small, hand-operated machine, a model so old he had never seen one like it except in the Bayport Museum. He brought out a length of hose and attached one end to the pump. Then he placed the opposite end over the rim of the barrel and moved the arm of the pump up and down.

Water began to run through the hose and splash into the barrel, which was soon filled up. Frank switched to a second barrel, and it also brimmed with water by the time the floor was dry.

"Good enough," Langton admitted. "Now, make yourselves useful on top."

The Phantom Ship

When the Hardys regained the deck, the night was still black but the storm was moving away. The rain had stopped, the wind was decreasing, and the waves were subsiding.

"We were lucky," Captain Parker told the crew. "We only caught the edge of the storm. Now, take your gear below. We have to get the *Samoa Queen* shipshape again."

When the Hardys returned from stowing their oilskins, members of the crew were already repairing the damage caused by the storm. One sailor was sitting on a yardarm halfway up the mainmast, trying to tie one end of a loose sail into place.

Captain Parker looked at Frank. "Frank Hardy, climb up the opposite end of the yardarm and help him. Lash the other end of the sail to the yardarm."

Frank clambered up the narrow ladder attached to the mast. Reaching the yardarm, he moved out onto it. He looked at the sailor across from him. It was Corkin!

"Do your job right," Corkin gibed at Frank. "Take your end of the sail and fasten it, and be quick!"

Frank did not reply. His end of the sail was flapping in the wind. To get hold of it, he had to stand up on the yardarm and reach out with one hand. His fingers had barely closed around the cloth when Corkin tugged hard.

Pulled off balance, Frank fell from the yardarm. Watching, Joe gasped as his brother began to plunge toward the deck!

But Frank managed to grab the yardarm at the last moment. He hung there as the mast rolled with the ship. Straining with his last ounce of strength, he got a foot over the yardarm and hoisted himself back up on it.

"You did that deliberately!" he accused Corkin.

The sailor grinned evilly. "You do not know how to work on the yardarm," he said. "That is all."

"I'll show you!" Frank challenged him. "I'll get the sail lashed before you do."

Both Hardys had shipped out as hands on a Coast Guard training ship, so Frank knew how to handle a sail. He seized the end whipping in the wind, ran a leather thong through its metal eye, curled the thong through a hook on the yardarm, and tied a sailor's knot to hold it firmly in place.

His chore finished, he edged over to the ladder. Corkin, looking discomfited, was still working on his end of the sail when Frank descended the ladder to the deck.

"Well done, Frank Hardy," said Langton, who had seen everything. "Corkin pulled the sail at the wrong time. But you have steady nerves and quick hands. I think you will make a whaler after all."

Grinning, Frank walked over to Joe and whispered, "Looks like your plan is working. At least we've got the first mate on our side. I hope he tells Captain Parker we're too useful to be dropped into the ocean!"

"I hope so, too," Joe said in an undertone. "But we're still in a terrible situation. We're—"

Captain Parker interrupted them by shouting, "Joe Hardy, come here!"

Joe hurried over to him.

The Phantom Ship

"Climb up in the crow's nest," the captain directed. "We are off Tahiti, and I want to know how close to land we are. I do not fancy piling my ship on a reef. Look sharp. If the *Samoa Queen* hits the coral, she will shiver her timbers!"

"Yes, sir!" Joe replied. He hurried to the foot of the mainmast, took hold of the ladder, and began to climb past the yardarms and the sails to the top of the mast. He slipped into the basket that was attached to it as a vantage point from which the lookout could survey the area around the whaler.

Because it was night, Joe could not see far. He strained his eyes to penetrate the murky darkness as the crow's nest swung in a wide arc above open water on one side of the ship, then over the deck to the other side. The wind blowing in his face made his eyes sting.

Why even ask *how* we can be near Tahiti, across the Pacific, he reflected. It's no stranger than anything else that's happened tonight.

"Ahoy up there!" Captain Parker shouted. "What do you see from the crow's nest?"

"Nothing but water on every side!" Joe called down. "Visibility is bad."

"It is good enough for you to see Tahiti!" the captain yelled. "And you had better alert me in time."

Joe resumed his vigil. Suddenly a dark outline showed against the murky background of the night, rising above the surface of the sea.

"That has to be land!" the boy exclaimed. "Ahoy down there!" he shouted toward the deck. "Land to the right! Land to starboard! Steer to the left! Steer to port! To port!"

On deck, Frank took up the cry. "Steer to port!"

To his horror, Joe heard Parker roar, "Steersman, steer to starboard!"

The *Samoa Queen* swung to the right and raced over the waves.

"Land directly ahead!" Joe cried in alarm. "Turn to port!"

On deck, Frank repeated the warning.

The Hardys were appalled to hear Parker bellow, "Full speed ahead!"

The ship hurtled onward. The dark outline above the surface came closer and closer with frightening speed. Then the ship struck the barrier with a shattering impact!

The mainmast snapped off with a terrifying crash, and fell down among the ship's rigging. Joe was thrown out of the crow's nest onto the deck!

He landed near Frank, who asked anxiously, "Are you all right, Joe?"

"I'm fine," Joe replied, faintly aware of the fact that he should be hurting but wasn't. "But I believe we're in big trouble!" He pointed to the captain, who was glowering savagely at them.

"You landlubbers are responsible for wrecking the ship on a reef!" Parker screamed.

"But I warned you that you were close to land on the starboard side!" Joe protested.

"And I repeated the warning," Frank reminded the captain.

"It does not matter. You are mutineers!" Parker

fumed. Turning to a group of sailors, he ordered, "Throw them to the sharks."

The crew swooped down furiously on the Hardy boys, seized them, and hustled them over to the rail. Suddenly the brothers saw a weird figure standing there by himself. It was the zombie who had lured them to the stern before and then had vanished into thin air!

He stared at them without expression, pointing over the side of the ship. Their captors hurled the boys in the direction he was indicating. But instead of splashing into the water, they landed on wood with a thump. Dazed, they stood up and looked around.

They found themselves in their motorboat, the *Sleuth*, and there was no sign of the *Samoa Queen* anywhere! A gleam of sunlight on the horizon revealed that they were in the Atlantic not far from Barmet Bay.

Frank and Joe stared blankly at each other for several moments. Then Frank pressed the launch's ignition. The motor roared to life! He tried the ship-to-shore radio. It worked perfectly.

"How come these gadgets are okay now when they weren't last night?" he mumbled.

"I don't know," Joe said. "All I know is I had a very strange dream—"

"About the whaleboat *Samoa Queen* going around Cape Horn in 1850?" Frank asked.

"Yes. Captain Parker's hostile sailors threw us overboard because we hit land—"

The Hardy Boys Ghost Stories

"Joe, that was no dream. We both had the same experience. And you know what I think saved us?"

"What?"

"The zombie no one else saw. He was our guardian phantom!"

THE
HAUNTED
CASTLE

The jumbo jet thundered eastward high above bil-
lowing white clouds that drifted across the Atlantic.
Through the window, Joe Hardy could see the coast
of Scotland.

"We'll be landing soon, Frank," he remarked to
his brother. "And then we'll find out what this
mystery is all about. Lord MacElphin sure was secre-
tive when he phoned us in Bayport."

"He was too nervous to say much," Frank observed. "There's obviously something strange going
on."

The Hardys were referring to the fact that Lord
MacElphin, an old friend of their father's, had called
Fenton Hardy and asked him to carry out an investi-
gation at MacElphin Castle in Scotland.

Mr. Hardy was tied up with an assignment for the

Federal Bureau of Investigation, so he had advised the boys to take the case.

"Be careful, though," he'd warned them. "Lord MacElphin doesn't get upset easily. Something dangerous must be going on at his castle. Still, I know you two can take care of yourselves. So go ahead and book the next flight to Scotland."

Frank and Joe drove to New York the next morning and caught a transatlantic jet to Europe. Now they watched as the plane circled around and landed at Prestwick Airport near Glasgow. When they had cleared through customs, they took a taxi and asked to be driven to MacElphin Castle.

The cabbie's face darkened as he started his car and moved rapidly into the Scottish countryside. "I cannot take ye to the castle," he informed the Hardys. "I'll leave ye at the gate and ye'll have to go the rest of the way on foot."

"Why won't you go to the castle?" Frank wanted to know. "Is something wrong up there?"

"Aye, you could say that. Something no man or woman should meddle with."

Joe's curiosity was stirred. "Can you tell us what it is?"

"It's the powers of darkness," the driver muttered hoarsely. "The witch's curse on the house of Mac-Elphin!"

The Hardys were startled by the outburst of the man, who turned off the highway onto a dirt road that ran through farming country. Then he resumed his weird tale of witchcraft.

"I do not know the whole story because it's one

nobody should pry into," he went on. "But I wish to tell ye this. The witch's curse goes back to him they called the Wicked Lord, the first Lord MacElphin, centuries ago. And it continues to this day. That's why I will not go near the castle."

He said no more as he continued into the countryside and finally stopped at a barred gate between two stone towers. One bore a plaque that read MacElphin Castle.

"This is as far as I take ye," the driver declared. He unstrapped their suitcases from the rear of the taxi and placed them on the grass. Then he took the money Frank handed him and, with a quick wave of his hand, left.

Joe tried the gate. It was locked, so he rang the bell. A buzzer sounded, indicating that the gate had been opened by remote control from the castle. The boys went through, and, carrying their suitcases, they trudged a few hundred yards through a spreading grove of evergreens to MacElphin Castle.

They stopped in the driveway and gazed up at the tall building made of large blocks of weather-beaten stone. A circular turret rose high over one corner, and from it, whipping in the wind, flew a flag decorated with a brilliant-white skull and crossbones against a background of jet-black.

"That's a pirate flag!" Joe exclaimed. "The Jolly Roger! People got out of the way in a hurry when they spotted it on the Spanish main!"

"But what has the Jolly Roger got to do with MacElphin Castle?" Frank was puzzled.

As he spoke the front door opened and a woman

stepped onto the flagstones outside. She was tall and thin with sharp features and a hard expression.

"I'm Mrs. Crone, the housekeeper," she announced. "You must be Frank and Joe Hardy. Lord MacElphin is expecting you. Come in."

The young detectives followed her into a large entrance hall, where a servant took their suitcases upstairs. Just like the housekeeper, he went about his chore with a downcast expression, as if he were afraid of something.

"This way," Mrs. Crone said tartly. "I'll show you to Lord MacElphin's study."

They followed her down a long hall, which was lined with portraits of former MacElphins. The faces appeared to frown on the Hardys as they passed. The brothers noticed that one spot was empty. A light oblong mark on the wallpaper showed that a picture had once hung there.

Frank was curious about the missing portrait. "Why was that one taken down?" he asked Mrs. Crone.

She scowled. "The last person to ask that question got such a fright that he left the castle and never came back!"

The boys shivered at her words. "What a mystery this is," Frank muttered softly to himself.

They followed the housekeeper up a staircase, past suits of armor flanking both sides. A couple of crossed swords decorated the door at the top of the stairs.

When Mrs. Crone knocked, Lord MacElphin came out. He was a wizened little Scotsman wearing a tartan kilt and a tam-o'-shanter on his head. The housekeeper introduced the new arrivals, then left.

The owner of the castle shook their hands and showed them to a sofa in his study. The room was illuminated by dim rays of sunlight filtering through a dark bay window. A heavy carpet muffled their footsteps.

The desk behind which Lord MacElphin sat down had a statue of a snarling wolf on one side and a smirking, gnomelike figure on the other. The center was bare.

"I'm glad to see you, boys," the lord began. "I need your help badly."

"We're here to give you all the help we can," Joe assured him. "Just tell us what to do."

"Before I do that, I'd better fill you in on the background so you'll know what you're up against," MacElphin commented. "No doubt you saw the flag over my castle."

"The Jolly Roger," Frank said.

"You were probably surprised to see a pirate flag," MacElphin went on. "Well, it was brought home by my ancestor, Rollo MacElphin. He *was* a pirate, one of the worst that ever traveled the Spanish main nearly three centuries ago!"

The boys looked at the man in surprise and he shrugged. "Rollo MacElphin sailed with Captain Kidd on his last voyage. Captain Kidd was hanged in the end, but Rollo MacElphin got away. He returned with enough treasure to build this place and gain the title of lord."

Joe chuckled. "That's quite a story."

"Aye. And Rollo always had a pirate's heart! They called him the Wicked Lord. He was a fellow who would stop at nothing to get what he wanted."

A thought occurred to Frank. "That's why his portrait was removed from its place in the castle hall."

MacElphin nodded somberly. "But it wasn't only his reputation that made me take it down. It was his face. Look here!"

The Scotsman pressed a button and a center panel in the top of the desk rose up on hinges. He lifted an oblong canvas out of its secret hiding place, turned it around, and held it so the Hardys could see it.

They were startled to be confronted by a horrible face glaring fiercely at them. The first Lord Mac-Elphin had matted hair, a flattened nose, a leering mouth, and crooked yellow teeth. One eye was covered with a black patch while the other had a cruel glint in it. In an upraised hand he wielded a sharp cutlass as if ready to swing it at anyone looking at his picture.

The Hardys shuddered.

"I see you don't like the Wicked Lord." Mac-Elphin grinned. "Visitors were always horrified when they saw this picture in the hall. So I took it down and now I keep it hidden in this secret compartment of my desk. I don't want to lose it because it completes the series of portraits of my ancestors since he became the first Lord MacElphin."

The present owner of the castle replaced the hideous picture in the secret compartment and closed the lid. Then he put his elbows on the desk, clasped his hands, and peered gravely at the young detectives.

"You're going to meet the Wicked Lord," he said darkly.

"How?" Joe gulped. "He lived centuries ago."

"He has come back," MacElphin replied in an ominous tone. "And now he's haunting the castle!"

Frank sat bolt upright in his chair. "You mean—a ghost?"

"Exactly. The ghost of Rollo MacElphin. There's no mistaking him. He looks just like he does in the picture."

"Then you've seen him?" Joe inquired.

"Aye. It began two weeks ago after I announced that, as I have no heirs, I intend to sell MacElphin Castle to a syndicate in Glasgow. That night I heard a weird noise. Someone was singing pirate chanteys in the cellar! I went down and, lo and behold, there was the Wicked Lord in the dungeon. When he saw me, he vanished."

"He must have scared you out of your wits!" Joe exclaimed.

"He did. A few nights later, when I was in bed, I heard chains rattling in the cellar. The sound drifted upstairs toward my bedroom. The next moment I saw the Wicked Lord carrying chains like the ones he used to fasten his sea chest in the cargo hold of his ship. The real chains, by the way, are still in the dungeon."

"And then he disappeared again?" Joe wanted to know.

"As soon as I looked up," MacElphin replied. "And then there was the night I came back from Glasgow. I saw the Wicked Lord standing on the turret under the pirate flag. He was glowering at me. Of course, when I ran up to the turret, he wasn't there anymore."

MacElphin broke off and shook his head as if trying to rid himself of the memory.

"Lord MacElphin, has anyone else in the castle seen the ghost?" Frank questioned.

The Scotsman nodded. "Mrs. Crone and Haver, my butler, have seen him. They also heard the sea chanteys and the rattling chains. My servants are now so terrified that they refuse to go near the cellar anymore."

"Have you tried to get help?" Joe asked.

"Yes. I hired a detective from Glasgow. He didn't believe in ghosts before he came here. I showed him the portrait and he kept the dungeon under surveillance the night he arrived. But then he saw the ghost and it frightened him so much that he refused to stay at the castle any longer."

"That must be the man Mrs. Crone told us about," Joe said. "The one who asked about the picture and got so scared that he fled from the castle."

"Suppose we see the ghost," Frank said slowly. "What do we do then?"

"I consulted the occult books in my library," MacElphin replied. "One says a ghost will sometimes talk to strangers from another country. That's why I called your father. I hope you're not afraid," he added anxiously.

The Haunted Castle

Frank shrugged. "We're not afraid, Lord Mac-Elphin. We just don't know what to expect."

"I can't tell you what to expect," MacElphin confessed. "I'm depending on you to decide what to do when you meet the ghost. I've made arrangements for you to spend tonight in a room opposite the dungeon. That way, you'll be able to hear everything. Haver will show you down there after dinner."

He summoned the butler to take the Hardys to their room. Haver was a big man with a mournful look. He talked about the ghost as he escorted them up the broad staircase to the second floor of the castle.

"I saw the Wicked Lord one night last week when I passed the dungeon on my way to the storeroom," he said. "I heard a weird noise, looked through the grill, and there he was! But he vanished when he saw me."

"What did you do then?" Joe inquired. "Did you go inside?"

Haver shuddered. "That was the last thing I would have done. The ghost gave me such a turn I ran upstairs at once. I haven't gone down there since then. I do hope you boys can get rid of the ghost!"

"We'll try," Frank promised.

The butler showed the Hardys into their room and then went downstairs. Frank and Joe sat on their beds and discussed the strange things they had seen and heard since their arrival in Scotland.

"There's a double whammy on this place," Frank declared. "First, the witch's curse that scared the taxi driver. And then the ghost of Rollo MacElphin."

Joe tapped a knuckle against his chin. "I wonder if there's a connection. We'd better ask about the witch before we meet the ghost."

When the dinner bell rang, Frank and Joe went downstairs. They met Lord MacElphin and Mrs. Crone, and the four had their meal together. It was a somber affair. Haver supervised with a doleful expression, and the maid who served appeared worried.

The conversation centered around the ghost. "I saw him in the dungeon," Mrs. Crone informed the Hardys. "I was carrying some vegetables in from the garden when an eerie sound made me look in. The phantom was there, uttering weird cries. Unfortunately, he disappeared when he saw me."

The Hardys questioned the housekeeper closely, but she could tell them no more.

Mrs. Crone doesn't seem as afraid as Haver does, Frank thought to himself. I wonder why.

Joe changed the subject. "Lord MacElphin, the taxi driver who brought us here mentioned a witch's curse on the castle. Have you any idea what he meant?"

"Mrs. Crone knows more about that than I do," MacElphin replied.

The housekeeper looked embarrassed. "It's just that I belong to the Village Historical Society," she murmured. "According to our records, a coven of witches used to meet on the land where the castle now stands. It is said that when the first Lord Mac-

Elphin built his home, depriving the witches of their meeting place, the leader of the coven placed a curse on it. But that's just an old superstition."

Dinner broke up shortly afterward. Lord Mac-Elphin retired to his study, Mrs. Crone went upstairs, and Haver led the Hardys down a spiral stone staircase to a passageway below. The butler took a torch from the wall. It was made of long, twisted fibers and was coated with pitch at one end. He lit the pitch with a pocket lighter and it burst into flames.

"This is a flambeau of the type used back in pirate days," he stated. "It's been a tradition, ever since the first Lord MacElphin, to light the dungeon area in the old-fashioned way."

Haver held the flambeau high in one hand, and it flared wildly as they moved along the dark flagstones of a narrow stone passageway. The Hardys felt eerie chills at the weird, twisting shadows thrown on the walls by the leaping flames.

The butler stopped at a massive wooden door pierced about three-quarters of the way by an iron grill. "This is the dungeon," he said. "If we followed the passage to its end, we would reach a door leading out of the castle into the vegetable garden."

He produced a large key from his ring, unlocked the door, and pushed it open. They went in and looked around.

The dungeon was a grim prison made of stone blocks. Near the ceiling was a heavily barred window. Handcuffs and leg irons were hanging on metal pegs driven into the walls. One peg held a couple of long, narrow chains.

"Those must be the ones the pirate used to fasten his sea chest with," Joe inferred.

"The same kind his ghost has been rattling around the castle," Frank added. "But now the ghost isn't here."

The butler game him an uneasy look. "He comes when you least expect him. So you boys had better be on your guard tonight. He might sneak up on you."

"We'll take turns sleeping and standing guard," Frank told him. "We do that often on our investigations."

"This investigation won't be like any other you've ever undertaken before," Haver warned.

"That's for sure," Joe agreed.

When the Hardys finished inspecting the dungeon, the trio left and Haver locked the door. They went into a room across the hallway, which was bare except for two cots.

"This is where you'll sleep tonight," the butler said. "If you can, that is."

He gave Frank the key to the dungeon. Then he forced the burning flambeau into a socket beside the door, handed Joe the lighter, and left.

The Hardys sat down on their cots in the darkness that was broken only by flames of the torch shining through the doorway. They listened intently, but not a sound reached them from above.

Suddenly the silence was broken by a loud thump in the passageway, and a stiff gust of air caused the flambeau to go out!

Frank and Joe bounced to their feet.

"The ghost may be in the hall!" Frank exploded.

The Haunted Castle

"And he may have blown out our torch," Joe muttered. "I hope we can see enough in the dark."

The boys rushed into the passageway and looked around. But they saw nothing in the dense gloom. Frank peeped through the grill in the dungeon door, but all was black inside.

"Joe, light the flambeau," he suggested.

Joe used the lighter to get the torch burning again. They decided to investigate the hallway, which ended at a wooden door. It was unlocked, and, going through, the brothers found themselves in the garden. They saw nothing out there and returned to their room across the dungeon.

"Maybe the door was open and blew closed," Frank speculated. "And that was the noise we heard."

"And the wind in the passageway put out the flambeau," Joe completed the thought. "Nothing spooky about that, if that's what happened."

They sat down on their cots again. Frank stretched out to go to sleep while Joe stood guard.

Suddenly a ghostly voice began to sing a sea chanty in the dungeon! The words told of pirate voyages and buried treasure:

The Jolly Roger flies on the Spanish main,
The pirate ship is sailing toward the land,
And Captain Kidd has brought his treasure back,
But who knows where he'll hide it in the sand?

As the strident tones rose higher and higher, Frank and Joe raced out of their room. Joe grabbed the flambeau while Frank unlocked the dungeon door. There they barreled into the prison cell.

They came to a skidding stop in the middle of the dungeon and stared bug-eyed at a wraith near the leg irons on the wall! The ghost was dressed in a pirate costume, had a black patch over one eye, and waved a cutlass. The face was that of Rollo MacElphin!

He broke off his sea chanty. Leering at them, he shrieked, "Hardys, leave the castle!"

The mention of their name startled Frank and Joe out of their trance.

"How do you know who we are?" Frank asked boldly.

"I know everything that happens here!" the specter replied.

"Why should we leave?" Joe asked.

"Because you are meddling in things that do not concern you! Leave now, or we will meet again!"

The outlines of the wraith became dim. Frank and Joe could see through it to the wall behind. They leaped forward with their hands outstretched, but the ghost had vanished and Joe found himself clutching nothing but one of the handcuffs.

The Hardys stared at each other in the flickering light of the flambeau.

"Frank, the ghost is for real," Joe muttered. "And he's threatening us!"

Frank shuddered. "I wonder what it means. Well, we'll be ready for him if he comes back tonight."

But the ghost did not return. In the morning, the Hardys informed Lord MacElphin.

"So, the ghost talked to you," he marveled. "But

since it threatened you, I'll understand if you boys want to go home to America."

Frank shook his head. "We came to do a job, and we're not about to be scared off."

MacElphin looked relieved. "When you see my ancestor again, try to find out why he's haunting the castle."

Joe suggested questioning the servants. "They may have heard something last night that will give us a clue," he said.

"Go ahead." MacElphin shrugged. "But the wind was howling so loudly that I doubt anyone noticed anything. I certainly didn't."

Frank and Joe began with the cook. Then they talked to the gardener, the gamekeeper, and the maids. They all had rooms in the attic, and all denied hearing anything.

Mrs. Crone was hostile when they approached her. "You two let the ghost get away last night!" she shouted. "You should go home!"

"Why do you want us to leave?" Joe challenged her.

The housekeeper looked down. "I don't want you to be in danger," she whispered.

"Then how do you suggest we get the ghost to stop haunting the castle?"

"Tear the place down!" She walked away without another word.

The Hardys were startled at her outburst. "I'm suspicious of Mrs. Crone," Frank declared. "I think she knows something, and she's afraid we'll find out what it is. We'd better keep an eye on her."

Joe nodded. "Good idea. But now let's search the castle. Maybe we'll find a clue somewhere."

Frank agreed and they investigated the building room by room. At last they arrived on top of the tower. Standing under the pirate flag, they could see over sinister woods where large black ravens perched on branches of tall evergreens. Their harsh croaking echoed dismally through the trees. In the distance was a small village.

Joe pointed. "We haven't found anything here," he said. "What say we try the village?"

"The local people may know something that might help us," Frank agreed.

The young detectives went downstairs again and walked through the woods until they reached the small hamlet, which consisted of a business center surrounded by houses. The Hardys stopped passers-by and inquired about the castle. But everyone they questioned looked frightened and refused to answer.

"You better go away," one man warned. "Even though we may know about the ghost at the castle, we don't want to admit it. Nobody wants to get involved."

Only the postmistress was willing to talk to them. "The village suffered when the Wicked Lord was alive," she explained. "That was centuries ago, but now people are afraid that his ghost may haunt them forever."

"Has the ghost been seen in the village?" Joe inquired.

"Not yet." The woman shook her head. "But you never know, do you?"

The Haunted Castle

Frank raised the question of the witch's curse.

"I have only one thing to say," was her reply.

"What's that?"

"There will be a full moon tonight!"

"What do you mean?"

But the woman would tell them no more. Instead she turned to a customer to sell him stamps.

Puzzled, Frank and Joe went back to the castle. "What's a full moon have to do with the witches?" Joe wondered.

An idea occurred to Frank. "Maybe there'll be a meeting tonight, Joe! Witches get together under a full moon, don't they? Suppose they gather on the castle grounds, near where they used to meet before the place was built?"

Joe became excited. "Could be someone in the castle is a witch!" he declared. "Mrs. Crone, for instance. She's been acting kind of strange all along."

Frank nodded. "We're supposed to hunt for the ghost, but we'll keep an eye on her at the same time."

That night after dinner the Hardys went into their room opposite the dungeon. Frank took the first watch while Joe tried to sleep.

About an hour later, Frank heard footsteps on the spiral stone staircase. Quickly he lay down on his cot, closed his eyes until he could barely see, and pretended to be asleep. The footsteps advanced along the passageway until they stopped at their door. The next moment, Mrs. Crone looked in!

Satisfied that the Hardys were asleep, she turned

and peered through the grill into the dungeon. Frank felt the hair rise on the back of his neck when he heard her speak.

"You are not here, Rollo MacElphin!" she intoned in a hoarse whisper. "Return soon!"

Then she continued walking down the passageway. Frank silently got up from his cot and shook Joe awake.

"It's Mrs. Crone," he whispered. "We'll have to follow her and find out what she's up to."

A moment later, both boys were on the trail of the housekeeper. She was just about to walk through the rear door of the hallway. The Hardys tiptoed behind her and soon found themselves in the garden bathed in the light of the full moon.

Mrs. Crone went straight into the woods until she came to a broad, open space between the trees. Hiding behind a clump of bushes, Frank and Joe saw several women already assembled in the clearing. They greeted Mrs. Crone as their leader.

Then they formed a circle around her and began an eerie dance, spinning slowly at first, but getting faster and faster as the tempo of their chant increased. Mrs. Crone stood silently, gazing at the moon.

Suddenly the dance ceased and the women went down on their knees, starting another rhythmic chant. "We are witches!" they cried. "We know the magic spells and will bring the powers of darkness down on anyone who tries to cross us!"

Finally the chanting stopped and the witches

held their hands out toward Mrs. Crone. She extended her arms to the full moon.

"The curse is on MacElphin Castle," she shrieked. "It shall remain until the castle falls! Then the domain of the witches will be ours again as it was in centuries gone by."

Frank nudged Joe. "That's why she said the place should be torn down," he whispered. "She wants to get their old meeting place back!"

"No wonder she's not afraid of the ghost," Joe added. "They're both occult."

After some more chanting and dancing, the witches disbanded. Most of them moved off into the woods, while Mrs. Crone headed back to MacElphin Castle with the Hardys dogging her footsteps. She went through the garden door into the passageway. Silently they came after her.

Again she stopped at the dungeon grill. "Are you there, Rollo MacElphin? No? Well, there is still time," she murmured.

"Time for what?" Frank demanded. "To haunt the castle till it has to be torn down?"

Mrs. Crone whirled around. Her eyes blazed in the dancing flames of the flambeau on the wall.

"I told you to leave the castle!" she hissed.

"We know why," Joe said. "You're a witch! We followed you to the meeting and saw everything! You want this land back. That's why you're so friendly with the ghost."

"Rollo MacElphin did the damage," Mrs. Crone muttered. "He must undo the damage!"

Frank looked sternly at the woman. "Did you

summon the ghost of the Wicked Lord to haunt the place?"

Mrs. Crone smiled, the corners of her lips curled slyly. "Ask Rollo MacElphin when you meet him!"

Frank made a quick guess. "Mrs. Crone, you slammed the garden door last night and made the flambeau go out. You thought we'd be scared and leave. You were worried we'd find out you're a witch; that's why you told us the curse was just a superstition."

"And you don't *want* to get rid of the ghost," Joe accused the housekeeper. "You just want to get rid of us!"

Mrs. Crone's guilty look showed the Hardys they were right. But she did not reply. Instead, she turned and hurried up the spiral staircase.

The boys let her go and went back into the room opposite the dungeon to resume their watch. Frank dozed off while Joe stood guard in the silence that blanketed the castle. Thinking he heard a noise in the dungeon, the younger Hardy quickly stepped across the room into the passageway and stared through the grill on the prison door.

Rays of moonlight slanted between the bars of the window, throwing shafts of yellow light across the floor. The handcuffs and leg irons, as well as the chains from the pirate chest, hung on the wall as before, but there was no sign of the ghost.

"I must be imagining things," Joe muttered to himself.

He was inspecting the flambeau to make sure it was burning properly when a furtive movement caught his eye. Startled, he swiveled around in time to see a large black cat scoot off along the passageway into the darkness.

They say a black cat brings bad luck, he reminded himself. I wonder if that was a ghost cat. Maybe Rollo MacElphin brought it back from a pirate voyage!

Ruminating over such thoughts, Joe returned to his post. He resumed his watch, sitting on the edge of his cot and straining his eyes and ears as the minutes ticked away slowly. Frank was still asleep.

Suddenly a noise brought Joe to his feet again. He awakened Frank as he heard the sound of metal striking stone!

Both boys darted across the room and out to the prison door. Through the grill they saw the Wicked Lord materializing through the wall beneath the window. The ghost swung his cutlass as he came, and the strange sound was caused by the blade striking against the blocks of stone!

Again Joe grabbed the flambeau while Frank unlocked the door. They burst into the dungeon, determined to corner the phantom, yet afraid it might vanish before they had a chance.

However, Rollo MacElphin did not disappear. He glared at them malevolently, his flattened nose, leering mouth, and crooked yellow teeth just as in the portrait.

The Hardys stopped a few feet away from the uncanny specter, who now spoke in an eerie voice that gave them cold chills.

"I have tested you before and you do not seem to

be afraid, strangers from another land. By the laws of the occult, I must speak to you! What I say may chill your blood. Do you dare hear it?"

Frank roused himself to a bold reply. "Yes. We do. Let us hear whatever it is!"

"I have been haunting this castle for nearly three centuries," the ghostly image said. "I was doomed to it by the witch's curse!"

"What is the witch's curse?" Joe asked, holding his voice steady in spite of the specter's evil look.

The ghost rested the cutlass in the crook of its arm and recited the lines in a harsh voice:

> Lord MacElphin at night shall roam
> Around the castle he made his home
> Until he returns the woods and land
> To the women of the witches' band.

The Hardys felt goose bumps as they listened to the ghost intone the weird verse. The uncanny creature went on, "The witch leader, an ancestor of Mrs. Crone, warned me not to build my castle on the meeting ground of her coven. But I scoffed at her. Therefore she placed the curse on me at the time of my death!"

The Hardys looked at each other. Both realized the clues of the MacElphin mystery were beginning to fall into place.

Joe faced the ghost. "So Mrs. Crone has power over you now," he surmised.

"Yes!" the specter snarled. "When she learned the castle was going to be sold, she ordered me to make myself visible to those living in it. Before that I was invisible, and only Mrs. Crone knew I was here."

"She thought if you were seen," Joe concluded, "the castle would have to be torn down, because nobody would buy it. Then the witches would get their meeting place back."

"And she ordered you to scare us away," Frank inferred. "But can't you escape from this witch's curse?"

The ghost nodded his head slowly, and something like a smile spread over his ugly face. "You are enabling me to escape right now!"

The Hardys were thunderstruck by the statement.

"How are we doing that?" Joe gasped.

"You are fulfilling a prophecy made by a wizard at my funeral." The ghost again recited some verse:

When a strange country help shall send,
Then the witch's curse will end.
When a hardy pair guards the dungeon door,
The specter needs to come no more.

Frank and Joe started when they heard the word "hardy." Both wondered if it could be a reference to their name. The ghost answered the question for them.

"I know you come from America, and your name is Hardy. And you had the courage to watch the dungeon for a second time after you saw me. Mrs. Crone thought the first experience would frighten you. She was wrong. You are hardy in nature as well as in name. The wizard's prophecy applies to you."

113

"What does that mean?" Frank wondered.

"It means you have released me from eternal doom! Mrs. Crone has lost her power over me and I can leave MacElphin Castle forever."

The voice of the apparition dropped to an eerie whisper and finally died away. The pirate's outline grew dim, and, as Frank and Joe watched open-mouthed, it faded back into the stones of the wall.

Frank rubbed his eyes. "Did we really see that, Joe?"

"Yes, we did! And we'll have some story to tell to our host in the morning."

When they recounted to Lord MacElphin what they had experienced during the night, he was amazed.

"Now Rollo MacElphin is gone for good?" he asked. "Are you sure?"

"Unless his ghost was lying to us, he's gone," Frank said.

"You boys are wonderful! You stayed despite the danger and saved all of us. Now no one who lives in the castle has to be afraid of being haunted anymore. But now I must deal with Mrs. Crone."

Summoned to the study, the housekeeper confessed everything. "I am descended from a long line of witches going back to the time when the castle was being built," she explained. "We have always known the ghost of the Wicked Lord was here."

"But he never showed himself before," the little Scotsman pointed out.

"That is true. I was the first with a chance to use the ghost to have the castle demolished and the meeting place of the witches restored," she said. "It had become necessary because of the impending sale. Better to destroy one castle than many houses that the real estate syndicate might have built on the property."

She nodded sadly and almost sobbed as she went on. "But I failed, and therefore I have lost my occult powers. I will go to Glasgow and cease to be a witch."

Now tears were running down her face and Lord MacElphin was too stunned to say anything. Mrs. Crone turned and left the study. Less than ten minutes later, she walked out of the castle for good.

Word that the Hardys had rid the castle of the ghost soon spread through the staff. The servants came to thank the boys and from then on went about their duties with smiles on their faces.

Haver shook Frank's and Joe's hands. "I was afraid that I could no longer stay on in my job," he admitted. "But now you have made it possible for me to work here as long as the master wishes me to."

"It must be strange to think you were living with a ghost all this time," Frank said.

The butler nodded ruefully. "And who would have thought Mrs. Crone was a witch? She and I have supervised the place for quite a few years now."

He shuddered and walked into the kitchen. The Hardy boys called the airport to reserve a flight, then went upstairs to pack their suitcases.

"We never got to use our room," Joe laughed. "These beds look a lot more comfortable than those cots in the basement."

"Well, we didn't spend much time on them," Frank pointed out. "Maybe we'll get some sleep on the plane home. I'm sure tired."

When they were finished, they went into the study to say good-bye to their host.

"Frank and Joe, you did a wonderful job, and I'll write to your father and tell him so!" MacElphin declared enthusiastically as he shook their hands and escorted them to the door.

Haver drove them to Prestwick Airport, and soon they were airborne over the Atlantic. They discussed everything that had happened to them in Scotland and agreed that they had been through an experience they could not explain logically.

"At least we had one thing going for us," Joe observed.

"What do you mean?" Frank asked.

"We had the right name for the wizard's prophecy. Sometimes it pays to be a Hardy!"

THE
MYSTERY
OF ROOM 12

"I don't know where you're taking us, but it sure is in the middle of nowhere!" Joe Hardy said to his father, who sat behind the wheel of the family station wagon.

Mr. Hardy chuckled. "The inn is quite isolated from the rest of the coastal communities," he admitted. "And the nearest airport is fifty miles away. But it's supposed to be a real nice place, so your mother and I thought we should try it."

Joe stared out the window at the deserted road, which was right next to the ocean. He saw a cliff rising up straight ahead of them, with a large white building sitting right on top. "Is that it?" he asked.

Mr. Hardy nodded. "It's called the Presidents Inn, because supposedly both Ulysses S. Grant and Theodore Roosevelt stayed there at one time."

"It's beautiful!" Mrs. Hardy cried out as they turned onto the steep road leading up to the hotel. "What a picturesque location!"

A few minutes later Mr. Hardy parked the car and the family got out. The inn proved to be a luxurious old place with a vast, sweeping lawn and thousands of blooming flowers still visible in the falling dusk.

"It looks more like the home of a wealthy family than a hotel," Frank declared.

"It probably was, once," his father agreed.

Joe suddenly stopped walking. "Even though it's beautiful, there's something ominous about it. I mean, it's so quiet, and a little eerie, don't you think?"

Frank grinned. "Your imagination is running away again, little brother," he said. "You must be tired."

Joe shot him a sidelong glance. Obviously they were not on the same wavelength in their impression of the place where they would spend the next few nights.

Just then a man came out to greet them. He was huge, with dark hair and bushy, beetling eyebrows.

"Welcome to the Presidents Inn," he said and picked up their suitcases with his large hands. "My name is Jacob. Please follow me."

Jacob led the Hardys into the lobby, where they met the innkeeper. He rose from his desk when he saw the visitors.

"Josiah Butler," he said, sticking his hand out for everyone to shake. "Yankee born and bred. Welcome to the Presidents Inn, Mr. and Mrs. Hardy, and your fine sons, too."

Josiah Butler looked every inch an Old Yankee. He was spare of build and didn't seem very talkative once the greetings were out of the way.

Joe studied the interior of the inn. There was plenty of shining old wood paneling, and the ceiling was crossed by heavy beams. The lighting was soft and dignified.

"Dinner is at seven sharp," Josiah Butler told Mr. Hardy when he had finished signing the visitors in. "Now Jacob will see you to your rooms."

The dark, sad-looking bellhop appeared again and led the way up two flights of beautiful, winding stairs. On the landings were pieces of Early American furniture, including a grandfather clock more than seven feet tall.

"Look at that!" Frank said and pointed to an antique winepress. "I've never seen one like that before."

"It dates back before the Revolutionary War," Jacob explained.

He ushered Mr. and Mrs. Hardy into room number 11 and pointed out that the boys would be next to them. There was a bathroom in between that opened to both rooms.

The boys took their bags and went right through the connecting bathroom into their room. It was large and airy and faced the ocean.

"Hey, this is great!" Frank said.

Just then Jacob came through the door to the

hallway. "Will you be all right here?" he asked. "You see, this is the first time we've opened this room since the place was converted to a hotel."

Frank shrugged. "It looks fine to me."

Jacob nodded. "Yes. Well, I hope you'll be all right. If you need me, just call. I'm never very far away." Somewhat hesitantly, he turned and left.

Frank and Joe looked at each other.

"What do you think he meant?" Joe asked.

"I have no idea. But he was almost apologizing that they put us in this room."

Joe nodded. "He gives me the creeps. In a way, this whole place—"

"Aw, come on, Joe. It's a great hotel. We'll have a good time, you'll see. Just look at the view out the window!"

Joe walked up to his brother and looked outside. The sight took his breath away. They were three stories up and the building sat right at the edge of a sheer cliff. A hundred feet below them the sea was lashing the boulder- and rock-strewn shore. The waves came crashing in, hit the rocks, and sent spray high in the air.

"That," Frank declared, "is almost scary."

"I'm getting dizzy looking down," Joe admitted. "But it is beautiful."

The boys could hear the mournful bass voice of a foghorn. A heavy mist had gathered far out at sea and was moving slowly toward the shore. A red-and-white-striped lighthouse stood on a long, slender finger of land that jutted into the ocean north of the hotel.

Frank broke their reverie at the window. "Come on, we'd better unpack. I want to take a shower before dinner."

Just then there was a knock on the door. The older Hardy went to open up and admitted a woman who announced that she was the maid.

Joe stared at her, barely suppressing a chuckle. She looks like the Good Witch of the East, he thought to himself. She even carries the right kind of broom.

The woman had a tooth missing on top, and her white hair stuck out like straw from the sides of her old-fashioned cap. Even her voice sounded like a raggedy cackle.

"My name is Elizabeth," she said. "I'll be cleaning your room, and I just wanted to know if you needed any extra towels or anything else?"

"No, we'll be just fine, thank you," Frank said.

The woman nodded and turned to leave. Then she stopped and looked back. "I guess you'll be all right here," she said. "Will you be all right here?"

"Sure," Frank said. By this time he began to feel strange, too. "Sure we will."

Elizabeth nodded and slowly walked out the door.

"I wonder why there is so much concern about us," Joe said when she had closed the door behind her.

"It is odd," Frank agreed. "Maybe we'll find out at dinner."

Shortly before seven they went down the hall and knocked on the door to their parents' room, and a few moments later all four Hardys entered the dining room. Josiah Butler had specific seats assigned to everyone, and they found themselves at his table, together with another family with two teenage daughters.

The girls were Amy and Susan Sheridan, and soon a lively conversation ensued while the guests ate a delicious meal of oyster stew and salad.

"Have you met the maid yet?" Joe asked Susan in a low voice.

The girl giggled. "I thought she'd ride off through the window on her broom! She scared Amy half to death."

"But she was really nice," Joe had to admit.

Susan nodded. "I know. It's just that she looks so weird. And she's not the only one!"

"I found a book with ghost stories in our room," Amy spoke up.

"Aye," Josiah Butler said. "Strange things happened around here."

"You mean they're true?"

"I don't know about all of them, but I sure know about some!"

"Oh, tell us!" Joe begged.

Josiah seemed pleased at that. With a crooked stem pipe that he couldn't keep lighted clenched between his teeth, he said, "I'll tell you one that I can prove, if you'd like!"

"Great!" Frank said, wondering how their eccentric host would prove his tale.

"This house," Josiah began, "was once owned by a wealthy sea captain. He had been a cabin boy at fifteen on a four-master that had gone all the way to

Shanghai, China, where the young man picked up a mysterious camphor-wood trunk. The trunk now sits in the upstairs hall; you may have seen it."

"I have," Joe said. "But where's the mystery?"

"Patience, my boy, patience." Josiah held up his hand as he continued. "There's more to come. In the year 1885 on a raging, howling February night, the captain, who by now sailed a windjammer named *Louisa K*, came back from a voyage to Africa. The ship appeared through the rain-drenched mists trying to make safe harbor with one broken mast and a crew ill with malaria."

"How awful!" Susan cried out.

"It was," Josiah confirmed. "Everything had gone badly for the captain. The malaria contracted on the West African coast had weakened him and most of his crew. A series of accidents, including the loss of a man overboard, and the shipping of water that had rotted much of the cargo, had the men muttering that the captain was a jinx."

"The poor man," Amy said. "Did he ever make it home?"

The innkeeper shook his head sadly. "I'm afraid not," he replied. "You see, this night his young wife went out on the widow's walk to watch the foundering *Louisa K*."

"What's a widow's walk?" Susan asked.

"It's a little balcony on top of the house," Josiah explained. "The sailors' wives would stand there to see out into the ocean as far as they could and watch their husbands come in."

"I suppose many of the men didn't make it, and

that's how the widow's walk got its name," Joe suggested.

"That's right," Josiah Butler said. "Anyway, there was the poor woman, seeing that her husband's ship was doomed. The wind at gale force broke the *Louisa K* up, taking with it the couple's chance for happiness."

"Did anyone survive at all?" Amy asked, her face sad.

"Some did," Josiah replied. "They told that the vessel was finally driven onto the rocks where the lighthouse now stands. At that point, the captain gave the order to abandon ship. He stayed on board to the last, helping injured and sick men to tie themselves to pieces of wood that would give them a chance of drifting ashore alive. And then, with all hands gone but himself, he retired to his cabin to await the end, playing his beloved flute. The sailors who heard it said they had never listened to such sweet music. Even people on shore, nearly a quarter of a mile away, swore they heard it loud and clear, the sound borne in by the wind."

Josiah Butler paused a moment, then continued. "Even the captain's wife heard it, walking her lonely parapet. She clenched her fists and wept, for she knew then that her man would never come home again."

"This story gives me the goose pimples," Amy said, shivering.

"And you haven't heard the eeriest part yet," Josiah went on. "Ever since that fateful day, in times of terrible storms, when men were in danger offshore here, there are many who swear they heard the flute again. They listened to the music of the dead captain, playing his ghostly melody from the bottom of the sea!"

"How scary!" Susan exclaimed.

Josiah nodded. "And there are those who looked at the inn's widow's walk on such nights and saw a figure, all in black, staring out to sea in perpetual longing for the love she would never see again."

There was silence for a moment, then Frank asked, "But what does this have to do with the camphor-wood trunk on the upstairs landing?"

"Ah, the trunk," Josiah said. "Ever since the captain's death, they say, the trunk gives off the smell of camphor, even though it's very old. You open it and see."

Frank and Joe were curious, and after the dinner party broke up, they stopped at the landing to investigate the trunk. It was a plain, light-colored box with precisely notched corners and metal hinges in the shape of dragon claws. Cushions had been put on top of it so that it could serve as a seat.

When the boys opened it, a strong scent of camphor met their nostrils.

"After a hundred years this is impossible," Frank declared. "Maybe old Josiah keeps something in it that smells like camphor?"

Joe pulled his pencil flashlight out of his pocket and shone it into the old trunk. There was nothing inside.

The boy shrugged. "Maybe Josiah sprays some perfume in here just before he tells his story to a new batch of guests," he said with a chuckle. "It's quite effective."

The boys closed the trunk and walked to their room. Frank was tired and went to sleep the moment his head hit the pillow; but Joe, for some reason, couldn't relax. He kept thinking of the sea captain and his wife. He lay on one elbow and stared out the window. The strong beam of the lighthouse swept in the direction of the inn every so often, and the foghorn issued a series of mournful warnings. Joe noticed that the fog was hanging over the coastline like a big blanket.

Finally the boy fell asleep. However, he woke up soon afterward to what sounded like the sobs of a child.

Joe sat up in his bed. The child let out a high-pitched wail, then caught its breath as it gulped for air. Then it continued crying.

That's funny, Joe thought. I don't remember any families with small children in this place. Seems to me the youngest person around is Amy Sheridan, and she's at least sixteen!

The child continued to cry, and finally Joe leaned over and shook his brother.

"Wh-whatssa matter?" Frank mumbled as he tried to remember where he was.

Just then the crying stopped.

"Ah, I heard this little kid crying," Joe explained. "Yet I can't remember seeing any small children in the hotel. Do you know of any?"

"No," Frank grumbled. "And I don't hear a sound. What'd you wake me up for?"

Joe sighed. "I was worried, that's all."

"You were dreaming. Now get back to sleep, will you?" Frank turned around and pulled his blanket over his ears.

But Joe lay awake for a long time, waiting to hear the sound again. Eventually he drifted off, but as soon as he did he woke up again with a start. This time there was no sound. He just had the vague feeling of a presence in the room, someone besides his brother.

Joe opened his eyes slowly to get used to the gloomy light that filtered into the room from the lamps that the hotel kept on all night outside. Then, suddenly, he saw the bathroom door opening slowly.

His skin began to crawl. He remembered that the door had squeaked before. Now there was no sound.

Horrified, Joe lay in his bed, watching the door swing wider and wider. Someone must have gotten into Mom and Dad's room, stolen their things, and is now coming in here by way of the connecting bathroom, he thought. No, probably worse than that. The ghost of the sea captain is coming to visit his wife!

Finally, the door touched the wall without the slightest noise. But no one was there! Maybe the ghost is invisible, Joe thought. He's probably standing above my bed right now, wondering who I am. Maybe he figures I did something to his lady and he'll strangle me!

With that, Joe shook himself out of his fantasy and, with a yell, turned on his bedroom lamp. Frank jumped out from under the covers and hit the floor in a defensive karate stance, his sleep-drugged mind convinced that they were under attack.

When his blurry vision cleared and he saw nothing but his brother, he sat down on the edge of his bed.

"What was all that about?" he demanded.

"The bathroom door opened silently by itself," Joe replied.

Frank groaned. "You were dreaming again!"

"No, I wasn't. Look!"

"We probably left it open before we went to bed," Frank said.

"No, we didn't. I remember closing it."

"So the wind blew it open. Will you cut it out, Joe? I'm trying to get some sleep!"

"Frank, I'm not kidding. Besides, the door normally squeaks. Here, I'll show you."

Joe got up to close the door. It squeaked loudly. He took the heaviest chair in the room and dragged it across the floor. Then he wedged it underneath the doorknob. "Maybe this'll help," he mumbled.

Frank was back under the covers. "If you wake me up one more time, I'll gag you!" he threatened.

"That's if the ghost doesn't get me first," Joe muttered and closed his eyes.

When he woke up the next time, he was treated to a ghostly doubleheader. He heard the soft sobbing of the child again. It seemed to come from nowhere and everywhere.

Then he looked at the bathroom door. It had swung all the way open, and the chair had been pushed back against the wall!

Joe jumped out of bed and walked over to touch the door and the chair to confirm he was not dreaming. Then he shook his head. "I'm probably dreaming this, too," he said aloud, but not loud enough to wake Frank.

Discouraged, he went back to bed. He brooded over the strange happenings until the sun came up. Then he fell asleep and didn't wake up until he heard his brother doing exercises in front of the open window. The chair still stood against the wall and the bathroom door was open.

"Did you move that chair?" he asked Frank.

"No. I figured you did. The door was open when I got up."

When they went down to have breakfast, Joe was wondering whether he had dreamed the whole thing. He asked his parents quietly whether they had opened the door. Both laughed. "No, of course not," Mr. Hardy said. "I broke your mother of the habit of checking on you boys when you were about five or six years old!"

"Joe's imagination was running wild last night," Frank said. "He woke me up three times because he thought he saw ghosts."

"Twice," Joe corrected meekly.

The family spent a pleasant day swimming in the heated pool, playing tennis with the Sheridans, and just lounging around, relaxing. But Joe did not really have a good time, because his thoughts kept drifting back to what had happened the night before. He had asked his brother not to say anything to the Sheridan girls, and Frank had agreed. "I won't embarrass you, don't worry," he said. And he kept his promise.

At dinner that evening, Joe was even more distracted, anticipating the eerie night ahead of him.

"What's the matter with you?" Amy prodded. "Don't you feel well?"

"Uh, I have a headache," Joe said. A little white lie was better than telling the truth and being made fun of, he thought.

When they finally went to their room, Joe was almost eager to get to bed.

"Now listen, little brother," Frank declared as he took off his clothes, "I don't care what you do with your ghost, but leave me out of it, all right?"

"Don't worry," Joe said. "I won't call you even if I'm in mortal danger!"

"Good. Pleasant dreams!"

Joe lay with the light out, listening to the foghorn's low notes seeping in from a distance. He waited and waited, but nothing happened. His visitor refused to come while he was awake. Finally Joe fell asleep. He woke up with a start when he saw the child standing in front of his bed.

It was a little boy, perhaps four or five years old. He was dressed in Victorian clothes, the kind people wore around the year 1890—a dark red velvet suit with a big bow tie around his neck, knee pants, stockings, and black shoes with buckles. He had a small birthmark on his right cheek. Tears were streaming down his face.

Joe got up on one elbow and started to get out of bed. The child was so real that he was convinced his family must be staying at the inn. But why was he dressed in such strange clothes?

Determined, Joe put his feet on the floor. For a moment he looked down for his slippers, and when he glanced up again, the little boy was gone! Vanished, as if he had never been there.

Joe sighed in despair and crawled back into his bed. I must be seeing things, he said to himself. Frank's right. I'm going crazy!

He buried his head in his pillow and went back to sleep. Suddenly he dreamt he was flying through space down the beam of the light flashing from the lighthouse. He looked to his right, where Elizabeth, the maid, was riding her broom and cackling. They were both swept around in great circles through the sky and then swooped low over the inn right past the grief-drenched wife of the captain on her widow's walk.

Then the witch was gone and Joe was back in the hotel. Jacob, the bellboy, was walking toward him. The little boy in the red velvet suit clung to his hand and was crying. As Jacob passed Joe, he stopped for a moment and said, "Will you be all right in this room?"

As Joe nodded, the sound of a flute filled his ears. It became so loud that the young detective woke up with a start!

The next morning at breakfast Mr. Hardy asked the boys if they wanted to go for a ride on the lake.

"I've rented a motorboat from the marina down the shore," he said.

"I'd love to!" Frank exclaimed.

Joe, who was tired from his ordeal during the past two nights, shook his head. "I think I'll just lounge around," he said. "I don't feel that great."

Frank shot his brother a sidelong glance, but he

said nothing. After everyone had gotten up from the table, he pulled Joe aside. "Did you have another run-in with the ghost last night?" he questioned.

"No, just crazy dreams," Joe replied.

By three o'clock that afternoon, it started to rain. A storm began to build and an hour later was in full swing. Mr. Hardy and Frank had not returned yet. Joe and his mother were worried, and Joe tried to call the marina from the hotel lobby. He found that the telephone lines were down.

"Why don't you go into town and call the Coast Guard," the manager suggested. "That's probably faster than driving there. They're about twelve miles away."

"Right!" Joe hurried outside and started off. He found a working telephone in a restaurant and called the Coast Guard, alerting them to the fact that there might be a disabled motorboat on the lake and the the phones at the inn were not working.

The firm voice on the other end of the line sounded reassuring. "We'll start looking right away. Don't worry, we'll find it. We'll let you know by shortwave radio as soon as we do."

When Joe returned to the inn, he found his mother in the Sheridans' suite. Everyone was nervously waiting for news. But none came, and the afternoon got darker and darker. Joe was feeling cold with fear. He listened to the foghorn, the crashing of the surf, and the howling of the wind. Any moment he expected to hear the sound of a flute amid the din.

Suddenly there was a knock on the door. Josiah stood outside, his Yankee face smiling broadly. "I just got a message from the Coast Guard," he said. "They found Frank and Mr. Hardy. Both are safe and sound at the station."

"Thank God!" Mrs. Hardy cried out, and Joe hugged his mother in relief.

"Their rudder had broken," Josiah went on. "A Coast Guard copter that managed to brave the storm picked them up. Anyway, because of the terrible weather they've decided to spend the night at the station and return in the morning."

Everyone cheered his words, and at dinnertime all the guests at the inn held a celebration in honor of the rescued sailors. Then the Sheridans, Mrs. Hardy, Joe, and some other people sat down for a game of cards.

Finally, about ten-thirty, everyone went upstairs to go to bed. Joe did not realize until he said good night to his mother that he would be spending the night without Frank in his room. The thought made him nervous.

He read for a while, but eventually he turned off the light and rolled over to sleep. He had just drifted off when he heard something banging. It seemed to come from the window. He leaned over to turn on the light, but there was no electricity. When Joe looked toward the window again, he saw the little boy standing in front of it. This time, the child was not crying. Instead, it was beckoning to him.

Joe bit his lip. As quietly as possible, he got out of bed, his eyes trained on the apparition. The little boy moved slowly toward the door, which opened all by itself. Then Joe went after the ghost to the second-floor landing.

There the child stopped in front of the camphor-wood chest; he motioned to Joe to open it, and the young detective obeyed. I suppose it's too heavy for him, he thought.

Then he stared in surprise. Inside the chest lay a flute! The little boy bent down and took the instrument. He looked at Joe and smiled. Joe was just about to say something when the apparition faded away.

Joe stared after his strange visitor in consternation. Then he closed the camphor-wood chest and returned to his room. He saw that the window shutter had become unlatched and was causing the noise that had awakened him. He stared out the window for a few minutes, then fastened the shutter and went back to bed. But before he could climb under the covers, he heard a loud *crash!*

Again, Joe bent over to try the light. This time it came on. He looked around the room until his eyes focused on a picture that had fallen off the wall.

It was a photograph which had been hanging amid a cluster of small pictures. Joe had not paid much attention to any of them. Now he got out of bed and picked it up. He gave a yelp of recognition. The photo showed the little boy, dressed as a miniature sea captain! From the brown sepia tone of the paper, the young detective could tell the photograph was quite old.

"That's him," Joe said out loud. "No doubt about it. It even shows the little birthmark on his cheek!"

The Mystery of Room 12

He put the picture on his night table, then sat up in bed for a long time. Finally, he fell asleep and did not wake up until the door to his room burst open.

Frank stood in the doorway. "Hey, Joe! Don't you ever want to get up? If you don't hurry, you won't get any breakfast!"

"Frank! Are you all right?" Joe cried out.

"I'm fine. They put us up on a couple of cots at the Coast Guard station and even gave us doughnuts in the morning. And look at that beautiful sunshine today! The storm has disappeared without a trace!"

Joe looked at the picture on his night table. "Not quite," he said.

"What do you mean?"

"If you promise not to make fun of me, I'll tell you."

Frank sat down on Joe's bed. "Go ahead, tell me about your ghost. I won't say a word."

Quickly, Joe filled his brother in on the night's events. Frank took the picture into his hands and studied it. "Well, perhaps Josiah will be able to give us a clue as to who this child is," he said. "Come on, get dressed, and we'll ask him."

Ten minutes later, the boys showed the innkeeper the photograph. "Can you tell us who this child is?" Joe asked point-blank.

The man put down his coffee cup and looked at the boys in silence for a moment. "So you've seen him," he said finally.

"Seen who?" Frank demanded.

"Eh, yep. Suppose you tell me."

Frank looked at his brother. "Suppose you tell him, Joe."

"I heard a little boy crying the past two nights," Joe said. "Same boy as in the picture. He came to our room. Last night, he didn't cry. He beckoned me to follow him to the camphor-wood chest and open it for him. Inside lay a flute. He took it and disappeared."

"Maybe that's the end of it!" Josiah burst out.

"The end of what?"

"Well, you see, there was a part of the story I didn't tell you. The captain who owned this house had a son. Your room was his room."

"And it was closed off for many years," Frank said. "Jacob said so."

Josiah nodded. "When I bought the place, I was told the room was haunted. The little boy came every once in a while and cried. But I've had the inn for quite a few years now, and no one ever heard anything, so we decided to finally open the room up."

"You could have warned us," Joe said. At the same time he thought of Jacob and Elizabeth, and how concerned they had been about the Hardys.

"I suppose I should have," Josiah admitted.

"I never heard a thing," Frank said. "I thought Joe was dreaming!"

Joe poked his brother in the ribs. "You're just not as sensitive as I am to the voices from the past."

"I guess not," Frank admitted.

Next time the boys passed the second-floor landing, Frank could not help but open the camphor-wood chest and cast a curious look inside.

"Joe!" he cried out in surprise. "The odor is gone!"

Joe shrugged. "Now that the little boy got his father's flute, even the chest isn't haunted anymore," he replied. "I'm glad I was able to help him, even though I have to admit he scared me half to death!"

BRUCE COVILLE'S

I was a SIXTH GRADE ALIEN

The fascinating and hilarious adventures of
the world's first purple sixth grader!

I WAS A SIXTH GRADE ALIEN

THE ATTACK OF THE TWO-INCH TEACHER

I LOST MY GRANDFATHER'S BRAIN

PEANUT BUTTER LOVERBOY

ZOMBIES OF THE SCIENCE FAIR

DON'T FRY MY VEEBLAX!

TOO MANY ALIENS

SNATCHED FROM EARTH

THERE'S AN ALIEN IN MY BACKPACK

THE REVOLT OF THE MINIATURE MUTANTS

THERE'S AN ALIEN IN MY UNDERWEAR

Published by Simon & Schuster   2304-06/01